Lock Down Publications and Ca$h Presents

TOP OF THE TRENCHES

CHARM CITY

Written By

Delmont Player

First Edition 2026

Printed in the United States of America

Lock Down Publications
P.O. Box 944
Stockbridge, GA 30281
www.lockdownpublications.com

Like our page on Facebook: Lock Down Publications
www.facebook.com/lockdownpublications.ldp

Stay Connected with Us!

Text **LOCKDOWN** to 22828 to stay up-to-date with new releases, sneak peaks, contests and more…

Like our page on Facebook:
Lock Down Publications

Join Lock Down Publications/The New Era Reading Group

Visit our website:
www.lockdownpublications.com

Follow us on Instagram:
Lock Down Publications

Email Us: We want to hear from you!

Chapter 1

"Damn! I wish this nigga would come the fuck on," Buttons said to herself as she waited in the basement of her mother's Section 8, three-bedroom home on Carey Street in West Baltimore. Buttons was waiting for Leroy, her mother's fiancé, to come into the basement. Leroy was late, as usual.

I hated fucking his ass after he fucked her. He took a long time to cum, Buttons thought. She was sure that her mother was sound asleep because she had peeped in on them before entering the basement.

"Damn, girl!" Leroy said, stepping off the last basement step, looking at his eighteen-year-old stepdaughter. She was a bad motherfucker, nice and thick in all the right places.

"You like, Daddy?" Buttons teased as she did a full circle in her mother's sky-blue Victoria's Secret boy shorts and bra set on with the matching six-inch stilettos.

"You tell me," Leroy retorted, pushing his sweats down. Fucking his stepdaughter turned him on to unexplainable heights. She was hands-down the finest white bitch he'd ever fucked.

"I guess you do." Buttons smiled, looking down at Leroy's long, black dick, dangling in front of him with what looked like dried-up cum along the length. She knew for a fact that it was traces of her mother.

Buttons wasn't crazy about Leroy, but she damn sure loved the effect she had on him. The way she could get anything out of him with some extremely slow, sloppy, deep throat made her feel powerful.

"Take everything except the heels off, and get over here!" Leroy snapped aggressively, stroking his long, thick dick as he eyed Buttons. Everything about her was intoxicating—the nails, her long, jet-black hair with the blonde streaks, the lip-gloss, pretty toes and all.

I love stretching that little young, tight pussy wide open. Leroy watched Buttons slowly remove her bra and boy shorts. At eighteen, Buttons was a bad little thing, standing five-foot-five, 130 pounds, blonde hair, with a grown woman's body. To top it off, the little bitch had the best head he'd ever had. What really made Buttons stand out, though, was the fact that she and her mother were the only two white girls who lived in the hood.

Buttons seductively made her way toward Leroy with a devilish grin and gently took his dick into her soft hands. To be honest, Leroy was far from her type, but he had money, and the dick was good, especially when he put that dope, black-honey pack, perk, BlueChew, or whatever he was taking for the night up in him. Yeah, two wrongs didn't make a right, but it damn sure still added to two.

"You like that, Daddy?" Buttons panted in Leroy's ear.

"Bitch, stop playing with me. You know what I want!" Leroy grabbed a handful of Buttons' long, blonde hair, wrapped it around his hand twice, and forced her down to her knees.

Buttons fell to her knees, knowing exactly what her stepfather wanted. Better yet, she understood what he needed. He needed all the things that she knew that her mother wasn't doing. He needed throat, and he needed ass. And he needed them both tight and bottomless like only she could provide.

Leroy slapped Buttons. "Open your mouth, slut," he ordered before slapping her across the face and spitting into her open mouth. "Stick your tongue out!" Leroy straightened up, tapped his dick on Buttons' juicy tongue, and slowly slid into her tight throat. "Good girl."

Buttons gagged and pulled back a little as if she didn't love the feeling of being choked, the feeling of her throat stretching out as she tried to deep throat Leroy over and over and over again.

"I fucking love nasty shit!" Leroy leaned forward and kissed Buttons in her mouth. There was nothing in the world more appealing than a nasty bitch who would do anything to please her man.

Buttons loved the way he looked at her, the way he towered over her like a giant. Buttons smiled up at him like a good little whore and remembered how it all began.

It all started one day when Leroy was fucking the shit out of Buttons' mother, Jessica—who everybody called Jess—in Buttons' room. They loved fucking in Buttons' room because she had those large mirrors that covered the entire bedroom wall. Jess loved seeing herself get long dicked. She loved seeing the contrast of their skin colors; it made her so wet.

The first time that Buttons stumbled upon Leroy and her mother, Leroy had been trying to get her mother to take it up her ass as he sat on the edge of the bed. It looked just like a black.com porn scene.

"I thought all white girls would do anything for their man," Leroy stated as Jess continued riding him as he fingered her asshole. He had never had a white girl until he met and fucked Jess. Afterward, he was hooked. He became crazy, just like all the others who'd had a taste of that white chocolate.

"W-We-We will, ahh. We will." Jess whined as she felt Leroy's dick in her lower stomach as his finger slowly went in and out of her little, pink asshole.

Now, Jessica's story was different. She'd been crazy about black men since stepping out on her husband with one three years before, and like so many before her, once she got her first taste of that forbidden fruit, she never stopped going back.

She began to lie, geek, and steal, all to please Leroy, and as a result, her husband of fifteen years filed for divorce, took more than half of what they owned, and disowned her and their daughter.

Jessica was riding Leroy hard as he sucked on her reddish-pink nipples and gripped her nice, white ass cheeks. Leroy used his left hand to lift Jessica off his dick. Then he used his right hand to hold his pussy-wet dick, and while looking in the mirror, he aimed for Jessica's pink asshole. It was slightly open from the finger popping, but still, Jessica whined as his dick stretched her asshole open.

The length was too much for Jessica. It felt like he was pushing a train into her back door. Jessica had to stop him. It was just too big. But to keep him happy, she got up and started sucking it.

It was at that moment, between earth and true heaven, that Leroy realized that his stepdaughter was standing in the bedroom doorway, fingering herself with one hand and sucking a banana with the other.

Leroy got lost in her water-blue eyes as he nutted harder than usual down her mother's throat.

Buttons mouthed the words, "Am I next?" and vanished before her mother realized she was there—or home, for that matter.

Buttons saw the way Leroy watched her, and she was tired of giving it up to little boys. Plus, Buttons knew fucking Leroy was the only way to get something from him. He always said no when she asked for money or anything else.

After Leroy and Jessica got Buttons' bedroom back in order, they went back to their own bedroom to lie down. However, Leroy's dick was still hard, and he couldn't get the thoughts of Buttons being so close out of his mind. All types of images flooded his mind.

Five minutes after lying down, Jessica was out like a light with a slight snore. Leroy slipped out of bed, crept out of the bedroom, and bumped right into Buttons just outside the bedroom door. The hallway was dark, but Leroy could clearly see that Buttons was naked. Her white skin had a glow to it, and although Leroy couldn't see her completely because of the minimal light, he was sure that she was put together. Her body was cut up like a younger version of Scarlett Johansson. Leroy instantly got hard.

Don't get it twisted; Buttons' mother, Jessica, wasn't hard on the eyes either. She had gotten a little old and jive busted up, but she was far from insecure. That was one of the things that Leroy had picked up on about white women after meeting Jessica. No matter how fucked up they were, they acted like they had the best bodies on earth.

He admired that confidence. Act like a queen to be treated like one. Black women were so self-conscious about things that didn't matter. They were worried about things like stretch marks, cellulite, stomach fat, and other things that didn't mean anything to a man. To be honest, the marks of giving birth were one of the sexiest things in the world to Leroy, another thing that Leroy didn't like about black women. They always made him feel like his dick was too small. 'Fucking Thots!' *he thought. White women couldn't care less. They just wanted to get fucked and cum.*

Buttons grabbed Leroy's dick right there in the dark hallway and said, "I am going to show you how this big motherfucker should be handled," before she dropped to her knees and started sucking him off right there, deep throating and gagging the whole way. After that, it was curtains.

Although Buttons was miles away from 'Virgin Street' and known as the easy white girl around the way, she'd never had a dick bigger than six, six and a half inches tops. She told Leroy it was her first time, but he knew better. Leroy became hooked the moment she started calling him daddy as he fucked her from the back right there in the dark hallway just outside her mother's bedroom door until he nutted.

"Yes, Daddy," Buttons submitted, approaching Leroy. Fucking him was a shot at her mother. Buttons felt like it was her mother's fault that she didn't have a relationship with her father. "Look at this big, black dick." Buttons took hold of Leroy's dick as she got down on her knees.

Leroy was looking down into Buttons' water-blue eyes. He grabbed a handful of her long, blonde hair and wrapped it around his fist.

"You like that, huh, bitch? Daddy's got a big ol' dick, don't he?" Leroy rubbed his dry cum-covered dick all over her pretty face and slapped her with it a few times. He had to get his money's worth every time he fucked her. He loved slutting Buttons out. He loved dogging her pussy because she always collected her money a day or two in advance.

Leroy had been paying Buttons since their first encounter, so he treated her like the white-trash slut she got paid to be. He did all the shit to her he couldn't do to her mother, and to him, it was like doing it to Jessica since they looked so much alike.

"Yes, Daddy. Can I put it in my mouth?" Buttons begged, sticking out her tongue, ready to eat the dick and get it over with. She was curious as to what Leroy was up to. He had given her an extra fifty dollars, so she knew his nasty ass had something freaky in mind.

"You like sucking Daddy's dick, don't you? Open your mouth, freak. Get my balls too!" Leroy barked, then continued when she followed his orders. "Look at me."

Buttons did as she was told.

"All you white bitches are the same, running around here, acting like you're too good for a nigga!" Leroy ranted. "But deep down inside, all you bitches are freaks. All y'all want is some black dick. Them white boys can't get deep enough, huh?" Leroy grinned. He was amusing himself. "You're a freak, just like your mother," he added.

"Down here disrespecting your mother like this with her dick all in your mouth, the same dick she just got finished riding and sucking. Your mother is the same way. She likes to eat this black dick after I cum from fucking one of my other bitches. She likes the taste of it."

"I love it though," Buttons revealed.

"You better keep it good and hard too then." Leroy dragged her toward him by her hair. "Now, eat up, bitch!"

As soon as, "Eat up," rolled off his lips, Buttons attacked his dick. *In and out. Gag. Spit. Deep throat. Spit. Gag.*

"Mmmhh." Buttons moaned from deep in her throat. "Yes, Daddy. You like how I suck this dick? Can you feel how deep my throat is, Daddy? I can still taste Mommy on you. I'm your slut. What do you think about that? Your daughter is a slut."

I hope this nigga hurry up and nut! Buttons continued to slowly worship Leroy's dick with her mouth.

Buttons had to admit, it made her feel good when she fucked Leroy. She loved the fact that he was her mother's man. It was just so forbidden, and it turned her on so much.

"Your mother can't handle this dick, but her head game is better than yours," Leroy taunted, knowing how that would get her going. He knew Buttons and Jessica were always competing with each other.

Taking her mouth off his dick but still holding it firmly, Buttons let it dangle in her face, inches from her mouth as she softly stroked his balls. She knew men loved that. Pre-cum was attached to her bottom lip and Leroy's dick. The E-pill that she had popped earlier was one hundred percent in full effect. Dropping her hands to her side, she began to deep throat the whole dick. Stopping again to talk shit, she said, "Come on, Daddy! Fuck my throat. I bet my mother can't give no-hands head."

Leroy started fucking Buttons' throat like he was in her pussy. Spit and saliva began running down his balls and dripping from Buttons' chin onto her neck and titties. "Damn, baby. Your mother ain't got shit on you." Leroy tilted his head back in ecstasy.

"I love your little freak ass. Lean your head back and look up at the ceiling so that your throat is going straight up and down," Leroy directed, adjusting Buttons' head. "Yeah, baby girl, just like that. Now, open that little throat up for Daddy. Make Daddy feel good. Make me happy. Oooooh!" Leroy couldn't help but close his eyes and moan as he slowly forced his dick down Buttons' throat while holding her head in place. "Good girl."

"Mmmm." *Slurp.* "Mmmmh." *Swallow*. "Sssss." Buttons moaned.

"I'm about to cum, bitch. Your mother loves to swallow this nut, but today, it's your turn." Leroy grunted with a moan just as he started nutting. "Ahhh, baby, damn! You better swallow it all too, bitch."

Buttons looked him right in the eyes as his thick nut went down her throat.

"Ahhhhh, you're a little nasty slut just like your mother!" Leroy snapped as his toes began to curl.

"Mmmh." Buttons moaned. If she wasn't anything else like her mother, she was definitely a cum-guzzler, so she became extremely hornier as the warm, slimy cum flowed down her throat.

"Go sit in that chair, and spread your legs." Leroy gestured toward the kitchen chair over in the corner of the basement.

"Yes, Daddy." Buttons stood up and took off her panties.

Leroy watched as Buttons removed her mother's boy shorts. Her little bushy pussy peeped at him from the back. *Damn! She got a phat little ass to be a white girl.* Leroy watched her ass cheeks jiggle as she made her way to the chair. Leroy made Buttons climb up in the chair on her knees as if he was about to hit it from the back.

"Come and get this pussy, Daddy!" Buttons spoke once she was stable in the chair. "And go easy. Mommy's in the house."

"I got this," Leroy replied, licking his lips. He loved how her pussy cracked open. It reminded him of a deep axe-chop in an Oak Tree. "I got you." Leroy bent down and started eating Buttons' pussy from the back. He knew she didn't really care if they were caught.

"Ooh, Daddy, ooh!" Buttons moaned. Leroy's tongue was all in her business. He was eating both her pussy and her asshole. The E-pill had Buttons on cloud nine. "Ahhhhh, Daddy, you don't be playing, do you? Mmh."

Leroy tongue-fucked Buttons for a good ten minutes. He punished her clit, nibbling on it and flicking at it with his long tongue. Leroy kissed the pussy lips softly and blew in the pussy, all the while, teasing the clit. He was giving Buttons long, slow licks, teasing her clit with the tip of his tongue. He would start at the bottom of her pussy lips and slowly lick upward. He started slowly pushing two fingers in and out of her pussy. Leroy had his fingers in a hook, hitting Buttons' G-spot.

At times, he would hold her pussy lips open and lightly blow on them. He licked all around her pussy and kissed her soft thighs. *Damn, I love the taste of a woman. There's nothing in the world like eating pussy.*

Buttons instantly started cumming when Leroy slipped a finger in her ass. He worked two fingers into her pussy and one in her asshole while licking and sucking on her clit for a while. Once Buttons had cum again, Leroy switched places with her. He allowed Buttons to crawl between and begin sucking his dick until it was hard enough for her to get on it.

"Hold up! I want that tight, little, white asshole of yours," Leroy revealed, ready to allow Buttons to ride him to death. "I told you that I wanted you to do something special," Leroy reminded, turning her around before pulling her in close so that he could guide her into his lap.

Buttons wasn't sure if she was ready for that yet.

"I don't know." Buttons reached back between Leroy's legs and gripped his dick. "Your shit is too big!" Buttons confessed nervously, trying to pull away.

Leroy held on to Buttons and pulled her into a bear hug. "Come on, baby girl, please," he pleaded, kissing her on the nape of her neck. "I promise to only put half of it in." Leroy snaked one of his hands around in between her thighs. "What do you think I gave you that extra fifty for?" He teased her clit.

Leroy knew Buttons was a true freak, just like her mother, so he continued to kiss Buttons' neck as he slipped his fingers in between the wet folds of her pussy lips.

"Ooh, so that's what the money w-was for? Mmmm," Buttons spoke with a moan. She was still on cloud nine.

"Don't I always look out for you? Please, just let me put the head in. I'll throw you something else," Leroy promised. His dick was pressed against Buttons' ass cheeks. "Come on, baby girl."

"I want another hundred dollars!" Buttons replied, and it was music to Leroy's ears. To be honest, he'd have given her another five hundred dollars at the moment, had she requested it.

"That's Daddy's little girl. Grab that towel over there," Leroy instructed, pointing over her shoulder, thinking of how he was about to punish Buttons.

"This one?" Buttons leaned forward to grab the fresh gray towel off the table.

"Yeah," Leroy confirmed. "Now, follow my instructions," Leroy directed as he began to direct Buttons. "Sit up some." He waited. "Okay, good… Now relax your ass muscles… Put the towel in your mouth… Bite down…." Leroy began to sound like he was playing 'Simone Says'.

"What? I don't want—"

"Shut the fuck up and listen," Leroy snapped, cutting her off. "I don't want your mother to hear you moaning. That's all."

Buttons shook her head and followed Leroy's orders as he spread her ass cheeks and took his finger, still wet with pussy juice, and inserted it back into her tight asshole.

Buttons arched her back as she felt the pressure as Leroy pushed in.

First, Leroy pushed the tip of his finger inside. He wanted Buttons to want it, to beg for it. Leroy began sucking on Buttons' neck. After he fingered Buttons' asshole a few times, he started to feel her asshole relax and get extra wet. He knew it was time.

Holding and jerking his dick, Leroy pushed Buttons down onto it with some force, instantly hearing her grunting and straining as he slid in. He started encouraging her to relax. With no more than two inches in, Buttons started zapping, trying to get up, but Leroy held on to her tightly, continuing to force her down onto his pipe. Buttons felt as if her ass was on fire. The leftover spit on Leroy's dick served to cool the inside of her asshole down a little, but the pain was still serious.

"Please, stop. It's too big!" she argued through the spit-wet towel that was still clutched between her teeth. She couldn't stop biting down on the towel even if she wanted to.

"Yeah, mmm, ahhh, slut. Your shit is tight." Leroy held her tight and paid her pleas for mercy no mind as he kept pushing three to four inches of his length in and out of her ass. Her moans were turning him on, and he was close to cumming. Buttons' ass was starting to loosen up and get extremely wet.

"Leroy!" Buttons' mother suddenly called from the top of the basement stairs as the door came open.

Leroy froze but knew she wouldn't come down the steps unless he told her to. The basement was his second room. "Yeah?" he answered, still fucking Buttons slowly.

"Mmh, Daddy. Ah, my god. That's right." Buttons moaned through the towel, excited that her mother was so close.

I got your man, bitch, Buttons thought as Leroy stretched her asshole open. *His dick all up in this ass. You can't keep him happy, slut.*

"How long are you going to be before you come back to bed?"

"I'll be back up in a few minutes," Leroy spoke while looking Buttons in the eyes before whispering to her. "You are my little bitch. Riding this dick while your mother is less than ten feet away."

Jessica was telling him something, but neither he nor Buttons heard a thing she said.

"I'm cumming, Daddy!" Shaking and moaning through the towel, Buttons dug her nails into his thighs, feeling, for the first time, what it was like to have an ass-gasm. Leroy always told her that he didn't care about her digging her nails into him since her mother did the same shit.

"I am too. I'm about to fill that ass with nut," Leroy whispered just before he started cumming. "Ah, shit. Damn, bitch! Freak-ass bitch."

Buttons had never truly had anal sex, a finger or two here, a dick head there, but never had she taken something as thick as Leroy.

After Leroy nutted, it triggered Buttons mentally, and she came again once she felt that hot slime, which seemed to feel cool. Leroy had Buttons clean him up as best as possible with her tongue and mouth before wiping himself down with a wet cloth and heading upstairs after kissing Buttons goodbye. He knew she would dip out the back door and show up at the front in about an hour or two, which was cool with him.

"Bye, Daddy," Buttons said in a very low, sexy voice. She loved teasing him. "I'll let you put the whole thing in next time, Daddy."

Leroy looked at her with lust in his eyes. *I should fuck her again real quick.* Leroy peered up the steps as if contemplating his next move. *Damn! This little bitch got me.* "We will see," he said and went up the steps on a mission to fuck the shit out of Jessica.

* * * * *

"Brittany! Brittany!" Jessica called from downstairs somewhere.

"Huh?" a half-sleep Buttons answered once she realized her mother was screaming her name. It had to be no later than nine o'clock in the morning.

"The phone!" Jessica shouted.

I know this bitch knew that I was sleep. I can't wait to move the fuck up out of her house, Buttons thought, picking up the phone.

"Brittany!" Jessica screamed again.

"I got it!" Buttons snapped, picking up the phone with an attitude.

"What's up, bitch? I know you aren't still in bed?" Keisha asked after she heard Buttons' mother hang up the other phone.

"Girl, bye. You know that I'm still in bed." Buttons yawned in Keisha's ear.

"There's only one thing that will keep a bitch in the bed," Keisha teased.

"Yeah, a nice summer day," Buttons revealed. "Shit, plus, unlike you, I'm trying to enjoy my last few weeks of summer," Buttons said.

"She must've gotten some good dick after we left," another familiar voice chimed. "Did that nigga eat it?"

Buttons instantly knew it was one of her other sidekicks. "Nichelle, bitch! You the one who fucked little-dick ass, telling Corey, from the Avenue," Buttons said before she and Keisha started laughing.

"Whatever!" Nichelle replied. That was one body that she truly regretted. "Anyway. What are we doing tonight?"

Keisha Paylor, Yusra Mohammad, and Nichelle Spencer were Buttons' three closest friends. Together, they made up their clique, 'Lucky Charms'. Keisha was Buttons' sandbox best friend. They did everything from beating bitches down together to fucking with brothers at the same time.

Nichelle had moved around their way in early 2015 out of Westport. Yusra had moved from New York in the early nineties and was raised on Catherine Street, near Westside Shopping Center. Yusra and Keisha went to school together.

At seventeen, Keisha was the youngest of the crew, but she damn sure wasn't built like it. Keisha weighed about 125 pounds, stood about six-three, had that caramel, light-brown skin with the golden-blonde hair, and walked like a goddess. Then there was Nichelle, the chocolate dime piece who stood about five six. Nichelle had more ass than titties, but that didn't stop niggas from chasing her all across the city. Finally, there was Yusra, the oldest of the 'Charms'. At twenty-three, Yusra was probably considered the baddest of the crew.

It wasn't that all of them weren't bad, because they were. They all had something that separated them from the rest of the crew, but Yusra was the perfect combination of Japanese, Dominican, and black. She had that sassy, exotic look. On top of that, she stood about six feet tall in heels and always strutted like a model in her stilettos.

"I want to go out. Shit, it's Friday, and a bitch ain't had no dick in a few days," Keisha confessed seriously.

"I am down with that," Buttons said.

"Y'all know I'm with it," Yusra added.

"So it's on then. Keisha, make sure you bring one of your older IDs because we are rolling with the twenty-five and older crew," Nichelle said, knowing Keisha always forgot her fake ID.

"Okay. But fuck that! Nichelle, are you going to tell Buttons who you fucked last night? Or should I?"

"Who you fuck last night, freak?" Buttons inquired, sitting up in bed, all ears. "Was it snitching-ass Corey?"

"Fuck no! I wouldn't fuck that bitch ass nigga again if my freedom depended on it."

"I would," Keisha admitted, laughing. "How do you think that I escaped the last indictment?"

"Who was it then?" Buttons asked, more curious than ever.

"Mind your business, bitch! Do I count all of your bodies?"

"Damn. What ever happened to *don't mention, don't ask*?" Yusra added her two cents.

"Girl, bye!" Keisha fired, ignoring Yusra's statement. "Tell her who you fucked, Nichelle."

"Y'all bitches so messy," Yusra fired.

"So who was it, bitch? Are you going to give us the tea or not? And I know that it better not have been Josh," Buttons warned in a joking yet serious way. Josh was a dude from over in East Baltimore whom she had a major crush on. Josh ran with Keisha's brother, Knocky.

"Don't nobody want Josh little ass."

"So, who was it then?" Buttons pressed on.

"Larry!" Nichelle confessed.

"You fucked Larry? The crazy nigga who went viral for throwing Christmas parties on Halloween? Larry High?" Buttons added his last name to make sure they were talking about the same Larry.

"Yep," Nichelle admitted without shame.

"Bitch! Ralph is going to kill you," Buttons fired. She couldn't understand why Nichelle would go out and fuck niggas when she had a good nigga at home—a nigga who got money too. It was always dumb bitches with weak game who fucked shit up.

"Girl, please. Ralph not crazy," Nichelle declared. "But let me tell you, that nigga Larry High got a baby arm between his legs. My pussy is still sore," Nichelle revealed.

"We want all the details." Keisha had always been curious about Larry High, but he stayed locked up so much she never got a chance to get the dick.

Nichelle went on to tell Buttons and them how she'd fucked Larry and sucked his dick. Then she went into graphic detail about how Larry High had eaten her ass as she came in loud squeals.

They went back and forth for ten minutes about the sex.

"Damn! That nigga a freak like that?" Buttons asked, wondering if she should give Larry's crazy ass some pussy next. She hated to eat after one of her girls, but the way Nichelle was bragging had her ready to say fuck it. Besides, it wasn't like she hadn't done it before.

"And guess what?" Nichelle teased.

"Just tell us, bitch." Keisha had her ear pressed to the phone.

"I'm tired of hearing this shit!" Yusra fired.

"What?" Buttons questioned, wanting to know the scoop.

"I let him put it in my ass," Nichelle said, licking her lips as she thought back.

"You slut!" Buttons yelled like she hadn't gotten her first taste of anal sex a few days earlier.

"Bitch, let me tell you, that shit is big. At first, it felt like he was breaking my back. The funny thing is, Ralph is crazy about that shit. He has been into that shit since he got locked up. He's been asking me to stick my fingers in his ass and shit. So, I'm not new to it. Plus, Ralph is big, but Larry shit is so fucking thick that my asshole had to stretch open to accommodate that shit," Nichelle explained.

"At first, I was scared when he kept running his dick up and down my ass crack, but I was horny as shit because Ralph is out of town. So I asked him to put it in my ass. I wanted to see if I could take it."

"Damn! Now you got me wanting to fuck that nigga now!" Keisha confessed.

"Girl, that's nasty," Yusra replied.

"Yusra, I know you're not calling anybody nasty," Nichelle said. There was a rumor around the way that Yusra had pulled a couple of trains. "That Muslim shit not fooling nobody except your parents, bitch."

"Girl, whatever! One thing about me is I only get nasty with my man." Yusra was a freak at heart, but only a privileged few knew it.

They talked about the neighborhood rumors and news, and after making plans to hook up that night, they hung up.

* * * * *

Nichelle, Yusra, Buttons, and Keisha pulled up into Element's parking lot on Baltimore Street, downtown. Nichelle was driving one of Ralph's cars. Buttons was in the passenger seat of the 2018 pearl-white Q45 Infiniti while Keisha and Yusra ran their mouths, as usual, from the back seat.

"Why would you drive Ralph's car, hoe-hopping?" Keisha questioned over the Cardi B song playing on the CD player.

"Because, unlike you, I didn't feel like jumping in no niggas car tonight," Nichelle said, looking around. The club was jumping. The outside line was almost around the corner, and most of the people were still in the parking lot, chasing niggas, money, or pussy. "And when you can get a nigga to buy you a car, or when you stop fucking for weed, holler at me. Maybe then, you can question me. Until then, fall back."

"Bitch, don't play. Don't act like your shit doesn't stink. You got platinum, but your dumb ass is still out here chasing gold." Keisha fired a few shots.

"Don't find yourself walking home."

"Whatever," Keisha said, knowing that Nichelle was telling the truth about her fucking for weed. Keisha couldn't get niggas to spend much money on her, but she was cool because her brother took care of her.

"Yeah. Whatever then," Nichelle repeated. Nichelle hated it when one of them spoke on something they couldn't do. Nichelle felt like she was the breadwinner of the crew. Truth be told, she was. All of them were fucking, but Nichelle was the one who could get anything out of a nigga—money, clothes, etcetera. Buttons and Keisha fucked for free, for the most part. Every now and then, they came off good. As for Yusra, she kept a nigga and was dumb enough to be loyal.

Nichelle didn't really have to freak—she had a whole nigga at home for real—but she was a stone-cold freak, point blank. She loved to fuck. That was why she would trip off of her first love. He wanted her to be down for him, but shit, she couldn't even keep her legs closed for her nigga in the streets. True, she loved him, and he did a lot for her when he was in the streets, but damn, how much did he expect? She answered the phone when he called, most of the time, sent photos from time to time, and put a couple of dollars on his books when she could.

"Nichelle, bitch! Your loose pussy ain't better than nothing up in here. Your game is just tighter. I give you that, but you're still too young to have your shit loose like that," Buttons said, laughing from the passenger seat.

"That's from her having all them damn babies," Keisha added.

"Nah. That comes from taking all that dick," Yusra corrected.

Nichelle knew that, although they were all girls, if she ever got into it with Keisha, she would have to fight Buttons too.

"My pussy got a stronger grip too," Nichelle said, knowing what Buttons was up to. "Let's get in here and shut this club down."

Keisha was the first to exit the car. Hands down, she had the best looks and body out of the whole crew, with crazy measurements. Keisha had on a black, body-hugging shirt that read 'Lucky Charms R Magically Delicious' across her chest in red, skin-tight, sheer Under Armour shorts that showed off her red thong, and red leather boots.

Buttons was the next to step out while Nichelle finished checking her makeup. Buttons was the white version of Nicki Minaj. She had on a black and white full bodysuit with no bra or panties, and some black patent-leather, knee-high 'Come Fuck Me' boots. Unlike Keisha and Nichelle, Buttons got a thrill out of showing her body off. They always said that she was thirsty, but she didn't care. She loved the attention.

Yusra stepped out, showing off her legs in some little, white, form-fitting shorts, but her outfit was still respectable. She had her long hair out with a tight, pink shirt and matching heels. Yusra had the appeal of a grown woman.

When Nichelle finally stepped out of the car, it was over. Any nigga that wasn't already checking for her made it his business to start. Nichelle had a way of making bitches grab on to their men. She wore a white tube top with her belly ring showing, blue leggings, and white, open-toed heels. They had the attention of all the caramel, chocolate, and vanilla candy chasers from that point on.

"I'm feeling the hate already," Nichelle warned, showing off her new silver, heart-shaped tongue ring as they started toward the front door of the club, fat asses shaking with each step.

They could hear the "damns!", "shorty phat as shit!", "I will pay for an hour", "I'll suck a bone out of that pussy!" and all the other comments as they passed dudes in the line.

"Hold up, shorty," one dude said, grabbing Buttons' wrist as she walked by, attempting to turn her around to face him. "What's up with you and your girls?"

"What's up?" Buttons asked, smiling, loving the attention.

"Sorry, boo-boo. We don't fuck outside of V.I.P.," Nichelle declared, coming up behind Buttons, squeezing her ass, and hugging her around the waist before snaking out her long, wet, soft-looking tongue to lick Buttons from her shoulder up to her ear before sucking on her earlobe in front of everybody.

"Mmh. Let's go, Snow White." Nichelle made Buttons' ass jiggle with a slap.

"Bye," Buttons whispered sexily as she followed behind Nichelle, Yusra, and Keisha. Buttons couldn't help but look at Nichelle's ass. Buttons had seen Nichelle and Keisha naked several times and had even sucked Keisha's titties and played with her pussy one night when they had a threesome with some nigga, fucked up off of the pills. Buttons had been getting wet from looking at women lately.

"That bitch crazy," Buttons said to Keisha as they watched Nichelle whisper to the bouncer.

"Come on, ladies." The bouncer opened the door and let them in after they flashed ID cards that read twenty-five, twenty-six, twenty-eight, and twenty-nine years old.

"See how easy that was, Keisha? The promise of pleasure will always move mountains. The thought of pleasure is worth more than the pleasure itself. All you have to do is plant the seed," Nichelle said, lying, knowing that she used her boyfriend's name.

"I'm going to go grab me a drink." Buttons headed for the bar.

"Cool, I see my guy, so I'm going to get us some E's," Nichelle informed.

"Do that," Keisha replied. She loved rolling.

Buttons and them crammed by the bar and waited for Nichelle to come back with the pills so they could roll. Yusra was the only one who didn't get high off anything unless you considered life. She did sneak a drink of 'Hen-Rock' every now and then.

"Now, let me show you how to take the spotlight. This is how I keep my man. Come on," Nichelle said, pulling Buttons and Keisha to the dance floor. It had been about an hour since they'd entered the club, and the E-pills had almost kicked in full blast.

Yusra watched from the bar as she slowly nursed a glass of Hennessy.

Keisha, Buttons, and Nichelle hit the dance floor like the LAPD hit 'Cleo' in *Set it Off*… Hard. Nichelle was grinding on both Buttons and Keisha like they were having sex. Nichelle kept saying it was to get all the attention in the club. But the more she tongue kissed them, sucked on their fingers and ears, rubbed her hands and shit, the more turned on that they gotl between their legs, and cuffed their pussies.

Buttons' pussy was throbbing like crazy, and the fact that she didn't have any underwear beneath her bodysuit was worse. The club's dark atmosphere was the only thing that hid the fact that her crotch area was wet. The E-pill had Keisha ready to fuck. Nichelle was rubbing all over her and whispering freaky shit in her ear.

When Nichelle started rubbing Buttons' clit through her bodysuit, that was it.

"Bitch, you better stop playing," Buttons managed to say softly, face pink with lust, walking off the dance floor. All Buttons kept thinking about was the last time she got all horny, fucking around with Nichelle and ended up with some dude over East Baltimore. Buttons still believed that Nichelle had gotten some money for that shit.

"What's up?" Keisha asked as she went up to Buttons and Yusra at the table.

"Nothing. Where's Nichelle?" Buttons asked, looking around.

"She went to get us some more drinks," Keisha replied. "My throat always gets dry when I pop them damn pills."

"Mines too," Buttons confessed."

"Who you telling? Them pills got my pussy on fire." Keisha swarmed in her seat. "So what are you getting into tonight? Or better yet, who's getting into you? I know you got a dick shot lined up." Keisha smiled.

"Please! I wish," Buttons said honestly. "I'ma go home horny, get 'Busta'," she replied, referring to her dildo. "And try to knock the bottom out of this pussy. What about you?"

"I'm trying to get crushed. I was just dancing with Dewey. You know that's my baby. That nigga dick game is on point," Keisha said, looking around for her dose of dick for the night.

"I thought that was Curtis and Deontay's little brother?"

"Yeah, it is. Remember when we were fucking with both of them?"

"Hell yeah! Did you see Curtis with him?"

"Nah, but you know I asked about him. He said Curtis is married, girl."

"Damn!" Buttons spat. She would have loved to hook up with Curtis again. It would have been just like old times. "I hate going out. Ain't no fun if you can't get fucked good at the end of the night." Buttons spoke the truth.

"You need to find one good, stay-at-home dick," Yusra commented.

"Here," Nichelle said, popping up out of the crowd with drinks in her hands before Keisha could respond. "Sex in the streets."

"Sex in the streets? Who named this drink? You?" Buttons asked, looking at it curiously. "Drink with us, Yusra."

"Girl, stop playing. I have already had enough. SayQuan is gonna kill me now. Y'all lucky I'm even out. I should be home with my man."

"You a good girl," Buttons said, wishing she had a nigga to be loyal to.

"Well, this is some new mix they got. This shit supposed to have you off the hook," Nichelle said. "Here. I got y'all another pill too."

"Well, let me drink mine! Give me my pill." Keisha held her hand open and continued after she popped her E-pill and downed her drink. "Wipe your mouth, Nichelle."

Buttons looked as Nichelle's tongue shot out of her mouth and licked up what Buttons thought looked like saliva.

I'm too damn horny.

"Thanks, girl," Nichelle said, looking right at Buttons and licking her lips slowly again.

Calm down, bitch. That's your girl. You're tripping. You're just horny. This bitch is not licking her tongue at you.

They chilled at the table for about another hour. Buttons' body was on fire, and it seemed like everybody knew it. Everything felt sexual. When they left the club, Keisha went and got in the car with Dewey. Buttons talked to Dewey for a minute, telling him to tell his brother Curtis that she said hi. The whole time Buttons was leaning into the driver's side window, talking to Dewey, Keisha kept cutting her off, telling her to either come with them or let them go while she rubbed her hand up and down the length of Dewey's dick. Buttons couldn't help but to look down at it a time or two. *I bet he's nasty just like his brother.*

"Come on, Buttons!" Nichelle gave her a knowing look. "We gotta go. Bye, Keisha. Have fun, girl."

"I'll see you tomorrow," Buttons said, backing away from the Lexus LS400 with one last look at the dick.

Damn! I need to get fucked. I'm going to fuck Leroy tonight for free.

"Love you, girl," Yusra said.

"Okay," Keisha replied as they pulled off in route to the Town House Motel.

"I need to stop over at my house real quick," Nichelle spoke as Buttons climbed into the car. "Yusra, I'll drop you off after we leave Buttons'."

"Nah, drop me off over SayQuan's house," Yusra replied, knowing that they were right around the corner from her boyfriend's house.

"Well, I will drop you off first." Nichelle had to pass SayQuan's house to get to hers anyway.

"Cool."

"Good, I need to use the bathroom anyway," Buttons said.

"Who was that nigga Keisha was with?"

"Slim's good peoples," Buttons said, leaving it at that. She knew Nichelle's freak ass might try to fuck him for GP.

"Buttons, do you want to run in and use the bathroom real quick?" Nichelle asked as they pulled up in front of Yusra's boyfriend's house.

"Nah, SayQuan look like he's ready for his girl."

"Okay, y'all," Yusra said, getting out of the car. SayQuan was standing in the doorway. "Buttons, call me in the morning too."

"Alright." *Damn! I wish I had a man like that.*

They drove in silence all the way to Nichelle's condo on Light Street, in their own thoughts. Buttons was horny ass shit. She couldn't sit still.

"Come on in and use the bathroom real quick. You need to get home and call up some dick, with your horny ass. I know that."

"What?" Buttons asked, knowing that Nichelle was on to her.

"Just come on," Nichelle said and shut the driver's side door, walking toward the condo. She had been fucking with Buttons all night, teasing her and shit.

Buttons followed Nichelle into the condo. Once inside, Buttons went to the bathroom. Buttons loved Nichelle's place. It was laid out. Buttons felt like she was cumming as she used the bathroom. Buttons came out just as Ralph came through the front door with two of his friends.

"What's up, Buttons?" Ralph asked.

"Ain't shit."

"Nichelle!" Ralph called, walking into the back.

Buttons wasn't feeling any pain. She could hear Nichelle and Ralph arguing. He was mad because she had his new car at the club with, as he called them, her young ass freak friends. Then shit got quiet, and Buttons could hear light, manly moans. Ralph's friends were standing around, looking dumb.

Look at these dumb niggas. Why would you come with your man to his girl's crib, knowing he is trying to get his? Niggas is so fucking dumb, Buttons thought.

"Yo, come on." Ralph came from the room about ten minutes later, followed by Nichelle.

"Buttons, do you want to stay the night? I can call you a cab, but it's late."

"You can't drop me off?"

"This nigga trying to fuck, so he sending his boys home. He doesn't want me to leave."

"Damn, bitch! That's fucked up! How are you going to leave a bitch hanging like that? I'll just go home. Call me a cab."

"Girl, you know how it is with these niggas when they trying to fuck." Nichelle talked as she walked off to call a cab. "I just want to make sure you are okay. You can stay if you want to."

"Nah, I'm cool. Get your dick, girl."

It had been about fifteen minutes, and the cab hadn't shown up yet. Buttons called back twice, and they said it was on the way. Buttons could hear Nichelle fucking like crazy. The walls were paper-thin, so it was like they were in the room with her. Her pussy started throbbing again. Buttons listened to moans, groans, bed springs, and wet, slapping sounds. Buttons couldn't help herself. She went to the bedroom door and slowly cracked it open enough to peep in. And what she saw blew her mind. Nichelle was bouncing on Ralph's big ol' dick on the middle of the bed.

That was it. Buttons went back to the front room and started playing with herself.

Damn, Nichelle! I know you said it was big, but damn. I ain't know it was like that.

Buttons started playing with her own pussy through her bodysuit, rubbing her shit in a circular motion. Buttons was painting a picture in her head. The E-pills had her in Lala Land. She never heard the cab blowing the horn outside. Between the moans, and her imagination running wild, she would've been lucky if she heard Nichelle or Ralph walk in on her rubbing her whole body through her bodysuit while lying on the floor.

Buttons was going crazy, listening to the moans while rubbing her pussy and shit. She had freaky visions playing out in her head while she played with her pussy. She saw herself being called into the room by Nichelle. Nichelle was on the bed with her legs spread wide open. Ralph was lying back, playing with his dick.

Nichelle got her to eat her pussy first, and the next thing she knew, she was sucking Ralph's dick while Nichelle held her head and told her to relax her throat. Then she was eating his cum out of Nichelle's pussy. Ralph was putting an E-pill in her asshole, followed by his dick. His dick opened her up like crazy. She was going ass to mouth, mouth to pussy, pussy to ass. Ralph kept telling her that her throat game was mean, and she told them that she'd never had it that big. Then Nichelle forced her mouth down on it again. Nichelle showed her how to deep throat a twelve-incher with no problem.

As Buttons started cumming through her bodysuit, she pictured Ralph standing over her so he could nut into her and Nichelle's mouths while Nichelle had three fingers in his ass.

"Mmmm!" Buttons got up after she came, lay on the sofa, and passed out. She felt so good as she slept.

* * * * *

"Buttons! Buttons!" Nichelle called from what seemed like far away.

"Huh?" Buttons still felt a high from the night before.

"You want me to run you home before I go to work?" Nichelle asked, looking at Buttons lying out across the couch.

"Mmh," Buttons replied and rolled back over.

"Bye, bitch!" Nichelle made her way to the door.

Buttons passed out again before Nichelle closed the door.

"Mmh, Nichelle, go ahead. Let me sleep." Buttons moaned as she felt Nichelle rubbing something across her face. "Stop, bitch!"

Buttons knew that Nichelle loved to play. She just wasn't in the mood for playing right then. She still felt weak. "Stop, Nichelle!" Buttons snapped, opening her eyes, coming face to dick with Ralph. "Boy, what the fuck are you doing?"

"Your little white freak-ass keep walking around here like you the shit. Bitch, suck this dick," Ralph said, sitting fully on Buttons' chest, trapping her arms.

"Get the fuck off me, boy! What the fuck is wrong with you?"

"Open your mouth, bitch! I heard that all white girls' head be fire." Ralph was rubbing his dick all over Buttons' pretty face. He was leaving pre-cum all over her lips, nose, and face. "Come on, yo. Y'all white bitches born to suck dick and take it in the ass."

"Mmh, ugh!" Buttons said without opening her mouth as she fought to get up. Ralph's frame was too heavy for her.

"Come on, white girl. Suck this dick. Let me feel that bottomless throat I've been hearing about." Ralph had waited for Nichelle to leave for work before he came out and found Buttons still lying across the couch. He had seen her peep in on him last night.

"Boy, stop!" Buttons pleaded through clenched teeth.

"Bitch! What? You think that you're too good for me?" Ralph got mad and started choking Buttons until her face turned bright red.

"Please! Don't do this. Nichelle is my friend."

"So? I don't give a fuck. Don't play with me, bitch! Suck this dick. And if you ever tell someone about this shit, I will crush your white ass." Ralph was determined to get his issue. "Now, open up that pretty little mouth of yours, bitch!"

Buttons reluctantly opened her mouth and felt Ralph push the head of his dick into her mouth and toward her throat. Ralph's dick had to be every bit of twelve inches, and he pushed in until he choked her and got her spit all over his dick before pulling out.

"Bitch, you better get into it. Make love to this dick. I heard about you," Ralph said as he grabbed a handful of Buttons' tousled hair. He pulled her head forward as he pumped his dick in his other hand, slapping and rubbing the saliva-wet dick all over her face. "Go ahead and eat, bitch!"

"Mmmhh." Buttons started moaning out of fear, taking the dick into her mouth.

"Aaarrrrggh! Oooooh! Ooooooh!" Ralph moaned as Buttons started to suck his dick like the pro he had heard that she was.

The E-pill was still in her system. "Awwwww!"

She sucked mindlessly, humming contentedly as she held Ralph's dick deep in her aching throat. Every time the extra-big head went down her throat, it seemed to hurt more.

"That's it, bitch. I knew your little ass was a freak!" Ralph barked as he forced his dick down her throat. Buttons gurgled as Ralph crammed inch after inch of his dick right down her throat. "Mmh, ah, ooh!"

Buttons moaned with dick in her throat. She started kissing and licking his dick when he pulled completely out. By then, Buttons was totally consumed by both female and E-pill passion.

"Put your head like this." Ralph wrenched her head back so that it was lying flat on the couch. He pulled himself up like he was doing a pushup, letting her hands free.

Buttons instantly grabbed his dick and started jerking it.

Damn, his shit is big. Buttons was loving that big, black dick. It was wet as shit from her throat spit. It had a sexy wetness to it, to her. Cum was leaking out onto her face. Ralph started pumping in and out of her mouth. He moved her hands out of the way and started fucking her face like her head was nothing but a hole. His nuts were smacking against her chin. Buttons looked like she had an Adam's Apple whenever he was fully in her throat.

"That's it." Ralph pulled back enough to let her breathe through her nostrils, then he pumped his twelve inches down her aching throat again. "Oooooh!"

He made her suck it for another five minutes, then he got off her chest. "I'm ready to fuck."

"Hold up!" Buttons was not ready to go there. For one, he was her friend's boyfriend, and two, his shit was big, and she wasn't sure if she could take it.

"Don't make me fuck you up, girl," Ralph said and slapped her. That was enough to kill all the fight in her body.

First, Ralph made Buttons ride him. She felt him in her guts. All she kept saying was "Please" the whole time. Then he hit her from the back like she had never been hit from the back before. Buttons felt like a virgin again.

"Ralph, please don't do this to me," Buttons said when she felt his jumbo dick head at her back door. "Please."

Ralph lunged forward, and Buttons winced as her tender, almost-virgin rectum was forced wide open, and sharp, thorny quivers of pain tore through her ass, and she gave a broken cry as tears started filling her eyes.

"Yeah, baby. Your shit is tight. I knew that white ass would be tight," Ralph said. He could see traces of shit on his dick as he gave her the full twelve inches over and over again. Buttons' screams only seemed to turn him on.

Buttons moaned, cried, and screamed as her aching asshole locked snugly around the wrist-thick root of Ralph's dick. "Please, take it out. Please. Stop. No. I can't take it. Please, Ralph, you're hurting me."

"Shut up, bitch!" Ralph brought down his big hand, slapping Buttons savagely across the milk-white slopes of her ass, leaving rosy-red imprints on the tender, white flesh.

Buttons was still screaming as her raw asshole was being violated. Ralph was pounding into her with no remorse, his dick digging into her rib cage. She knew something would be wrong with her. There was no way her ass would be the same. Buttons was happy that at least the quivers of pain in her ass were rapidly fading.

"Aaarrrgggh! Oh my god, please! Ouch! Please!"

"You love black dick, don't you?" Ralph asked, pounding harder. He was long-dicking her with force. "Say it."

"Please, Ralph!" Buttons cried.

"Say it, bitch! Say that you love black dick." Ralph reached forward, grabbing her hair and twisting it around his knuckles.

"I love black dick! I love black dick!" Buttons cried out in a yell.

"I knew you did. All you white bitches do. Y'all bitches run around here like y'all racist, but the whole time, all y'all want is that black dick." Ralph slapped Buttons' wriggling, white buttocks hard before digging his fingers into her white flesh, leaving more red marks. "That's all you want, ain't it?"

"Please don't tell Nichelle."

"I won't. Now throw it back."

"Aaarrggh!" Buttons moaned and started pushing into Ralph, trying to feel the dick deeper.

"That's it. Yeah. Shit."

Buttons felt something pop in her back. "Oh my god, my back! Ralph, my back!"

"You cool." Ralph continued hitting that ass.

"Come and suck it," Ralph said, pulling out of her ass slowly with a pop about three minutes later.

Buttons could feel air enter her asshole and knew from the draft that it was wide open. She reached back to feel her tender rectum, and three fingers went in her hole with no problem. *Oh my God. I will never be the same.*

"Come here!" Ralph said, holding his dick. Ralph couldn't have cared less that her asshole was just sitting open. "It'll be easier for you to shit now."

Buttons could see long, thin streaks of cum on his big, shining dick as she took his dick into her hand to suck it. She started sucking him off as a means of getting it over with.

"Stick your fingers in my ass!" Ralph barked and moaned when Buttons complied.

"Mmmmh! Yes, baby. Just like that. Do it faster." Ralph was thinking of his homeboy, the enforcer who had been fucking him since they had shared a cell together up in the old jail out in Hagerstown, Maryland. Since then, it was the only way Ralph could cum. He had to have something in his ass. "I'm about to cum."

Ralph nutted on Buttons' face and in her hair. Buttons just stayed there and let the cum run down her face. Ralph jerked his dick, pushing out the last little bit of cum on her lips. Buttons was still fucking his ass with her fingers. She was disgusted not only by the act but also by the smell of shit. Buttons hated 'Homo Thugs' with a passion. *Gay ass nigga.* She couldn't understand why gumps faked like they were men. Cum was running down her neck when there was a knock at the door.

"Don't move, bitch!" Ralph walked to open the door ass naked. Buttons was too scared to move. Ralph opened the door, and in walked the two dudes from last night. "It's show time, bitch! Yo, this bitch is the truth."

Buttons stayed at the house another good two hours, getting dug and dogged out by Ralph and his two homies. They passed her around, taking turns on her, having her all at once, while making her try shit she had never heard of. After some time, Buttons had an out-of-body experience. She was no longer there; her mind was somewhere else as she was raped over and over. All she kept thinking about was how she was going to get even with all of the people who wronged her.

Chapter 2

Cutt-Annex, Jessup, Maryland. August 2018

"So, you're telling me that this chick wrote you off the internet?" Rayven asked his cell buddy as they were looking through his photo album.

"Yeah. Shorty bad too. Ain't she, man?" Moon asked. He had just moved into the cell with Rayven the night before, after coming off lock-up. Moon, whose real name was Marcus Alexander, was a five-eight, wild, twenty-something-year-old, light-brown-skinned, bald-headed nigga from Cherry Hill, who loved playing basketball. He was doing fifty years for second-degree murder. Rayven and Moon were waiting for the doors to open for morning recreation—dayroom, big yard, etcetera—so that they could go out and hit the phones and shit.

"Yeah, she's cool. I might get on that shit," Rayven spoke, thinking of how he always thought the pen pal shit was a fluke. He only knew a few dudes who really met a winner off the net. He knew there were some good women out there, but most of the internet chicks just loved playing games and using niggas as a pastime.

"You better jump on this. You might meet wifey," Moon said as he watched Rayven look at his girl. He had been fucking with her for about eighteen months.

"You got an application?" Rayven asked, not believing he was really going to go through with it.

He had heard so much about that internet shit. Gumps had been writing niggas, acting like they were women, and some more crazy shit. *Shit, fuck it. Maybe I can meet a chick to tell me a bunch of lies.*

"I got you when we come back in."

Rayven was a forty-year-old, young-looking, big, six-three, 243-pound, light-brown-skinned, pretty-boy type of nigga with good hair when he wasn't wearing his signature bald head. He had been down for nine years on a murder case, in which he pulled the trigger on one of his right-hand men. It was a simple case. Smallwood, Rayven's partner, had started snitching, and Rayven hated snitches. However, Rayven was forced to shoot his other long-time friend Zelda, first for encouraging Smallwood to snitch, and second for cooperating himself.

Before Rayven could get to Smallwood, he snitched. Rayven ended up with a sentence of life and twenty years in prison.

"Yeah, make sure you get me. I got an old photo from the good days, and I'm going to use my state pay to jump on that joint." Rayven didn't have any help from the outside. His mother, sister, and daughter would've given him the world, but he refused to accept it. Rayven used to get help from his younger brother, Lamar, before he started serving out a ten-year sentence for parole violation.

"Okay, fellers, you got five minutes to get somewhere!" the correctional officer yelled as the cell doors on the tier opened.

"Oh, shit! That's shorty that was working last night. Her name Hopkins, right?" Moon questioned, fucking with his cornrows, trying to look presentable.

"Yeah. That's shorty." Rayven stepped out to meet his chess buddy, another older cat who had been down for close to forty years, named John-Boy.

Ms. Dhaka Hopkins was all that and then some at twenty-six years old, five-five, and 135 pounds, with a mean body that contained a 24-38, nice ass, and some 32-C cups. Ms. Hopkins, or Dhaka, as Rayven called her when no one else was around, was a brownish redbone with a gap you could see through with her legs closed.

"Good morning!" Hopkins spoke as Rayven made his way past her to enter the dayroom.

"What's up, shorty?" Rayven replied, trying to be slick. Although Rayven didn't fuck with police, there were a few females he went for, and Hopkins was one of them. Rayven had known Dhaka as a child. He was from Cherry Hill, in South Baltimore, but he used to run with Dhaka's father in South Baltimore's pig town. They used to pull off stickups on white boys. Dhaka lived in the same house off Scott Street that she grew up in. After Dhaka's father was killed in a stick-up gone bad, Rayven changed neighborhoods and went on to start getting money on the other side of Baltimore Street in West Baltimore.

"Ms. Hopkins, not shorty," she corrected firmly, slowly, in front of three co-workers who were helping her pat (search) down the inmates for weapons as they entered the dayroom.

"Yes, ma'am." Rayven nodded, respecting her authority.

* * * * *

"Check, old man!" Rayven said to John-Boy, moving his rook to John-Boy's king, knight two, threatening to end the game.

John-Boy's face never showed any sign of emotion as his bishop came from Rayven's queen, bishop three to take Rayven's rook and put his king at ease. Rayven couldn't take his bishop, because John-Boy had it protected by his queen, the most dangerous piece in the game. "I'm cool under pressure, youngster," John-Boy said, knowing that, although Rayven had just started playing for real, he would beat him soon. Rayven was one of those kinds of people who had to be the best at everything they did.

"Damn!" Rayven said, acting like he was mad. His plan was to take John-Boy off his game.

"I know. Don't trip, youngster. It won't be long now," John-Boy spoke, seeing his next move to take the game. "Checkmate, Pops! Checkmate!" Rayven brought his queen out of what seemed like nowhere and set it right in front of John-Boy's king with the knight protecting it.

"I can't believe you got me with that. I slipped up."

"That's all it takes," Rayven said, knowing the truth of his own statement. In chess, like in life, each man makes the best move for himself. Sometimes that move costs him more than he planned to lose.

"You want to run it back?"

"Nah, we can play again tomorrow," Rayven replied. "I'ma sit on my win."

"So, what's up with your cell buddy? I know you don't really take to too many youngsters."

"Shorty cool. He's from out Cherry Hill Gramly but used to hang on Edmondson Avenue also," Rayven answered.

"Does he know that bitch Smallwood?" John-Boy asked, referring to Rayven's old hustling partner.

"Yeah. He said that him and some dude named Whitey, from Edmondson and Bright, got the Avenue on lock. Bitch nigga out there spending my money," Rayven said, laughing and thinking of the kid he raised in the game. "He's out there living good as a coward, while I'm in here dying as a man. Where is that written in the game's handbook?"

"Don't worry. The tables will turn. They always do. You can still look at yourself in the mirror," John-Boy assured him. "Did he say anything about him being a rat?"

"Nah, it's like nobody believes that shit, but I educated him." Rayven knew that he had done his part in exposing Smallwood. The coward had testified in Rayven's Zelda trial two and a half years after he snitched on their African drug connect. "That money makes motherfuckers go against the codes of honor. These rats have penetrated every form of the game."

"Yeah, you're right about that, but they are still rats at the end of the day. They can never shake that. When they are remembered, it will be for the dishonor they brought to the game—but men, they will be remembered for the honor they held."

* * * * *

In the cell that night, Moon looked at Rayven's photo albums as he read over the website information. The website, 'StillStanding.Com" was created and rin by a couple of ex-cons out of Washington DC, by the names of Anthony Fields and his partner, Buckey. They checked your paperwork, questioned your history—amongst both your friends and foes—before posting your ad. Rayven knew that it was saying a lot when even your enemy still gave you respect.

"I like this joint. It's like a newsletter too."

"Yeah, they honor a man and shit on a rat every month," Moon revealed.

Rayven flipped the ad over to see the last page. It had a large photograph of some guy on the back. Scribbled beneath the photograph in bold letters, it read 'Stand Up Man'.

"Yeah, I like this joint," Rayven admitted again.

"Do you know who that is on the back?"

"Nah." Rayven shook his head.

"Lemon Bullock, good man." Moon paused for a moment, wishing that he was in the streets when shit hit the fan. "He was like a brother to me."

"What happened?" Rayven looked at the photograph again.

"Not really sure," Moon said honestly. "All I know is that this rat-ass nigga named Hitler from up Longwood got jammed up for the Zelda."

"Yeah, I think I'ma jump on this joint and see what happens." Rayven wanted to change the subject. "I'm about to write my letter now."

"You got to fill out a money order, too, for twenty-five dollars," Moon reminded him.

"Yeah, I'ma do that in the morning."

It was one o'clock in the morning when Rayven finally finished rewriting his ad letter for the tenth time. He didn't want to say too much, but he also feared saying too little. Rayven was self-educated, having only finished the fifth grade in school, but on anything you asked him, 99 percent of the time, he knew about it and could answer your questions.

Rayven had decided to put his ad up for two years.

Rayven peeped up on the top bunk and saw that Moon was out cold, so he clicked the light off and lay down.

No matter what or who someone was in prison at night, they were alone. Truthfully, most dudes lost their minds when it came to solitude. Only the strong could live with themselves.

Damn! Shit had been going good, then Smallwood went and snitched and fucked everything up. Rayven had to get him. The sucker had only gotten knocked with a little weed and aired all of their dirty laundry. And for the life of him, Rayven still couldn't figure out what the fuck Zelda was thinking, trying to protect a rat? Rayven wasn't hearing any of that shit she was talking about "he not telling on you'. Shit, if Smallwood told on the connect, the nigga who helped him get money, he'd damn sure tell on the nigga who was in the way of him keeping it all.

Everybody acted as if Rayven was the bad guy because he'd moved on Smallwood, but he didn't give a damn. He did what he had to do. He set two traps but was only able to catch one rap.

Rayven lay in his bed, listening to Creed on his MP3 Player in his headphones. At the time of Rayven's arrest, their dope 'Power' was crushing the Avenue. Still, shit had to be dealt with because any nigga or bitch that knowingly protected, dealt with, or didn't expose a rat for any reason—money, drugs, freedom, etcetera—wasn't real. In the courts, it was called conspiring. In the streets, it was called 'birds of a feather, flock together'. If you weren't killing it or exposing it, let it be, because anything other than that was just as bad, if not worse.

Rayven had wanted to exterminate Smallwood once he confirmed he was responsible for their drug connect getting arrested by the Feds. Zelda felt like it was bad for business. Her thing was 'why hit Smallwood when they were all getting money?' Rayven couldn't live with the fact that one of his men had put a nigga in prison. He felt like, fuck all the money. He couldn't sell his soul, so eighteen months later, he made his move, but his timing was off. His plan was to hit Zelda first, but Smallwood showed up at the wrong time and saw everything unfold. The last thing Rayven said to Zelda was, "In this game, integrity is priceless; either you have it, or you don't." In the end, Rayven fell victim to the same problem he tried to rid the world of.

* * * * *

"Listen to this, Moon," Rayven said the next morning while Moon was brushing his teeth and getting ready for morning recreation. They had been back from breakfast for about an hour. Rayven always went to breakfast when they had eggs. "I'm looking for a friend to share thoughts with. Someone that's real and not afraid to be herself…"

"Yeah, that's tight," Moon said after he finished reading the entire letter before choking as he brushed his tongue.

"It's on then. I kept it simple."

"That's how you got to do it. All the other dudes be on there saying all kinds of slick shit. You just got to be real."

"Yeah. Men don't attract what they want. They attract what they are," Rayven said, getting ready to brush his teeth. "Here. Grab this," Rayven said, passing Moon an extremely sharpened piece of steel.

"I got it." Moon accepted the homemade knife Rayven passed to him. Moon knew that Rayven stayed strapped. He'd been asking him for some steel for a while now, never knowing when shit might jump off. It was everyone for themselves in prison because the police sure weren't going to help you

"That's you," Rayven said, knowing how bad a nigga needed some steel in prison.

"Good looking'." No questions needed to be asked as to where it came from or how it got there. In prison, some shit was just never asked.

"No problem. Turn the music on."

"You need some rap music up in here." Moon hit the play button on the MP3 player, and Creed came on.

"You keep pumping that white-boy music."

Rayven just laughed as he started brushing his teeth.

"Okay, gentlemen. You have five minutes to get somewhere!" CO Hopkins screamed as the cell doors opened. It was business as usual.

"Yo, Moon, what are you doing today?" Rayven asked. He had seen Moon talking to a known gang member in the dayroom the day before, while he was playing chess, and forgot to say something to him about it.

"I was thinking of running some ball in the big yard."

"I'm about to go run the yard with John Boy. Look, man, I ain't trying to be in your business, but I saw you hollering at Jungle in the dayroom. That ain't for you, soldier." To Rayven, Moon seemed like a young G.

"Nah. It ain't like that. That's my man. We were on lock-up together," Moon jive barked. He hated when the older niggas acted like they were his father or something.

"I didn't mean nothing by it," Rayven replied, picking up on his attitude. "I was just saying that leaders are like eagles; they don't flock. You always find them one at a time."

"I feel that. But trust me, it's not like that. I do me. I am nobody's toy soldier. That's that buster shit, for them buster ass niggas."

"Enough said."

* * * * *

"Yo, you crazy as shit!" Moon said. He was listening to Rayven tell him a story about getting chased by the police.

"This was like '91. Yo, I was running for about fifteen minutes. The police chump was on my heels. You know how long Fulton is, right? I hit Fulton after running up Edmondson Avenue, then I cut across the street and hit Harlem. Yo, I was out of it. By the time I got by the school on Monroe Street, I couldn't run anymore. I cut through the alley and ran right up into somebody shit. The back door was open. I had lost the police by then, somewhere around like Harlem Park."

Moon was laughing hard as shit by then. "Stop playing, Yo. I can't see you running up in somebody house in the hood. What were you thinking?"

"I don't know. I was trying to get the fuck away. I knew if they caught me, they were going to fuck me up. Look. Anyway, I comes up in the joint, and this lady start screaming like crazy. I couldn't talk, because I was out of breath, so I just pulled out a roll of money, trying to tell her to take it, but my chest is on fire. I can't breathe or nothing." Rayven was holding his chest to show Moon how he was. "Yo, shorty's son comes down the stairs and goes nuts."

"What?" Moon said as if he couldn't believe it.

"You have to understand. All he heard was his mother screaming. Yo, disregarded the money and got right with me in there. No rap. This little nigga dogged me too. Plucked me up, then dragged me through the house, and threw me out on the back steps. I couldn't even fight back; I was so tired. All I got to say was that I was getting chased, and I was trying to offer them some money."

"Hell no, Yo! Nah, on the real?" Moon asked, laughing hard as shit, picturing Rayven's circumstances. "You let that shit go?"

"Hell no! I got myself together, went back down the way and got some little soldiers, and we went back to that nigga house. I told his mother that I was sorry before finding out where he was, and I went down there. This nigga wasn't out, so I fucked up one of his homeboys. Shhiiit, I couldn't let that go," Rayven confessed.

In prison, niggas loved to go down memory lane. Sometimes, memory lane was all that they had to keep them in the streets.

"Yo, I got one for you. I'm over this chick house, right?" Moon started telling a story of his own.

They went back and forth for about two hours, then lay down to get some shut-eye, hoping the next day would hold something good.

* * * * *

"Fuck that! I'm hitting this bitch when we come out!" Moon barked as he paced the floor of the cell. Moon had just had some words with one of the kids on the tier in the kitchen while they were at lunch. "Did you see that nigga mugging me?"

"Stabbing Slim ain't going to prove nothing," Rayven assured Moon. Rayven knew the kid was no threat to Moon. The kid was scared for real. "He don't want that work."

"Nah, man, that nigga always got his face twisted up."

"Moon, 95 percent of the time, when a dude is always acting hard, like he's ready for whatever, like he's looking for war, most of the time, they're usually trying to make up for something that happened in the past—an act of cowardice. They know that one day their past will catch up to them, so they try to make it unbelievable. A man doesn't have to act hard. It's in his energy. You can just tell, even when he's acting soft," Rayven said.

"Man, it's like he is trying me, mugging me and shit like he thinks I'm a sucker or something. I'ma beat his ass."

"That's more like it. Everybody don't deserve that knife. When you pick up that knife, it should be to kill a nigga, not just to punish him." Rayven spoke nothing but the truth, knowing firsthand how a lot of niggas picked up knives and made the mistake of not finishing the job. "Just slap the shit out of him."

"I got him." Moon was calmer now. "How do you stay sane?"

"Time has frozen in my world. Everything stopped the day I was arrested. I let the youngsters have their way. This is not back in the day, when young dudes came in and listened to any and everything old dudes had to say. It's a new day. I respect these youngsters. If I don't like them, I don't fuck with them. But I respect them. I try to stay away from these crabs. These niggas don't want you to make it. If they see you getting out, they pull you back in. But I'm cool as long as they don't cross that line. I know they're not cut like me."

"I feel you. Why do you fuck with me?" Moon asked, really wanting to know. He had heard that Rayven didn't fuck with too many young niggas.

"Honestly, because I see that same fire in your eyes that was once in mine." Rayven didn't tell him that he reminded him of his dead twin brother, Raymond.

"Hey, Mayo, let me holler at you for a minute," Moon said to the East Baltimore fat boy.

"What's up?" Mayo asked with his mug still bent.

Mop! Moon slapped the shit out of Mayo. "Bitch ass nigga! You want some work?"

"Hold up! Yo, I haven't never disrespect you!" Mayo put his hands up in surrender.

"Get your whore ass off this tier before I put that knife up in you!" Moon said, slapping Mayo again. *Wop!*

"What's going on?" Mayo touched his face. Everyone could see that he was scared as shit. "What did I do?"

"You think niggas not hip to your bitch ass? You think niggas don't know that you told on the dudes over East Baltimore? You are a straight bitch! And you got about two minutes to get off the tier before I fly your sucker ass up out of here!"

Rayven was laughing hard as shit as Mayo walked off the tier. *I go for this little nigga!* Rayven thought, watching Moon.

Moon had truly just played a dangerous game.

In prison, sometimes, the strong would appear weak. You had to know your opponent, but Moon was a warrior. So, had Mayo wanted some trouble, Moon surely would've given it to him.

"Now look at this hot bitch!" Moon said as they watched the CO come on the tier, looking for a suspect to arrest behind Mayo's bitch ass.

"Why do you say that?" Rayven questioned.

"Because this bitch acts like a cop and shit."

"Acts?" Rayven repeated. "That nigga not acting. He's a CO. His entire job is to be hot. Don't ever forget that." Rayven knew a lot of dudes forgot that when COs let them get away with one thing or another.

"That's why he got fucked up last month," Moon said, laughing.

"Nah, he got fucked up because he played pussy and jumped out there with the wrong dude, but nevertheless, he got fucked."

"He'll learn when a nigga put that knife in his bitch ass."

"Sometimes, that's the only way to teach them. Some people only understand violence."

They went about the rest of the day as normal. Two dudes started fighting in the dayroom, but that was business as usual, so they didn't get locked down.

* * * * *

"So, what happened to her?" Moon asked, referring to Rayven's girl. They were locked in, talking about relationships. "Why did you let her go?"

"Because I realized that I had to stop trying to make something ugly out to be beautiful. It takes a strong woman to hold her man down, or as my cousin likes to say, 'hold a man up' in prison. A special woman and a lot of women just don't have what it takes."

"Damn! These bitches are shady."

"Nah, it's not that. All women aren't like that. Some women really love their men, but they're not built for the storm. Most dudes that go to prison in a relationship fall apart, but when you meet a lover in prison, that's something special because it costs a lot to love a prisoner."

"What about when you hook up with your old folks?" Moon asked.

"That's special too because it means more now. It means that she's really for you. When your people leave you while you're in, it means she's not really for you. Like when you're blessed with a soldier from the door, you know it. When a female stands and rides with her man, she's more than just a woman. Any woman that holds her man, brother, cousin, etcetera, up, and doesn't fold under the pressure is a superwoman," Rayven said, very familiar with how only a few women kept it real when their men were down and out. Most women loved being able to come and go in and out of a guy's life when it suited them. Women wanted to have their cake and eat it too. They felt like, because the guy was in prison, they could treat him however they wanted to. But a rider is a rider, and a man knows when he has one.

"Me, I'm cool just knowing that she's there. That's why Pooh and I don't have too many problems."

"That's how love is. Love has a power of its own. Love is the only power capable of conquering the heart. Remember the movie *King Kong*?" Rayven asked.

"Yeah."

"That's what love can do. Love can conquer both man and beast. Love is a force. Love drove that gorilla crazy about that white woman. Some people say that supposed to have represented the black man in America."

"Get the fuck out of here." Moon burst out laughing.

"You're laughing and shit, but I'm serious. They said the same thing about the *Curious George* cartoon. That was supposed to be the clueless black man following the white man around, being civilized."

"So, you're telling me that King Kong the gorilla and Curious George the little monkey represents the black man?" Moon was trying to read the serious look on Rayven's face.

"Absolutely. All that shit had a hidden message in it."

"That's crazy."

"America is crazy. But that's another story," Rayven assured, ready to change the topic before they ended up going down a rabbit hole.

"But anyway, like I was getting at, love doesn't allow men to abuse loved ones or burden them. Men do for themselves unless they really can't. Men don't ask, accept, or take nothing from their loved ones unless they really have to, just like you." Rayven spoke from observation. He had not seen or heard Moon talk about hitting his family up for money yet, like most young niggas who kept their hands out, always asking their family for shit.

Moon just shook his head. He felt Rayven. He hated having his hand out. It wasn't like he was well off or anything. It was just that he could always take care of himself. He was in prison for taking care of himself. He was a survivor. If shit got too bad, he knew how to put his gangster down and press the countless busters out. Besides, men knew how to survive and live off the land, and they enjoyed giving instead of taking.

"I know one thing else that's deep," Moon said.

"What?"

"Your pockets because you are drinking that coffee like it's going out of style. How the fuck do you drink that shit every day like that?"

Laughing, Rayven replied. "It's a man's thing."

"Yeah, an old man's thing."

"Shit, young dudes be drinking coffee too."

"Yeah, faking like they're old. Seventeen like Brandy, wanting to be down."

"Well, why do you wear your pants hanging off your ass?"

"That's the style."

"That's the style? Your pants hanging off your ass is the style?

"Yeah, that's how we wear our clothes," Moon defended.

"You can't possibly want me to respect that. Everybody is snitching now. Are you going to get with that style too?" Rayven asked and instantly saw Moon's face twist up.

"Come on. You know what I mean."

"Honestly, I don't. You got booty bandits running around here, and to them, I'm sure it looks like an invitation."

"I wish one of these bitch niggas would try me."

"I wasn't saying it like that. You're a man, and I know you'll deal with whatever like a man. All I'm saying is that you don't need to have your ass hanging out. Anything can jump off, and you need to always have your boots tied tight, and your belt strapped strong."

"I feel that." Moon knew Rayven was right.

"Listen, if I say that a nigga be in the police face too much, I'm not saying he's a rat. I'm just saying that the longer you talk to the police and ain't getting shit done, the more room it leaves for error." Rayven explained.

"A convict should never talk about another convict, what's going on in the jail, or why another convict did this or that. So, if you ain't talking on some real relationship shit, then what the fuck is you talking about? Niggas get relaxed with these police. She laughs, she smiles, and next thing you know, it's, "She likes me." Then you all in the bitch face, talking about nothing, and before long, you slip up," Rayven expressed. "The longer you're talking to or dealing with a person, the more your trust builds. I don't care who you are. It's human nature."

"That's why, if I had a female, I wouldn't even be around her. I know these niggas be lying on their dicks. Why would a bitch fuck one of these niggas that's always in their face? Shit, a nigga like that, and he ain't even getting the pussy yet? Imagine how that nigga would be if he got the ass."

"You have to be different. You have to stand out. Women crave strength, but they disrespect weakness. However, though, they are evil. They are the best that ever did it and got away with it. Eve broke Adam. Helen started the war of Troy. Women are master manipulators. Especially here. They get offered dick thirty times a day, trust me. These women have babies, so it ain't nothing you got that can hurt them. But you can make them feel good. When you meet a woman who is honest and knows what she's capable of, you and her can come 360 degrees together."

"Yeah, that's why I stay to myself around here, just in case I get chosen." Moon smiled. "Plus, I got Pooh anyway, and I think she's going to bring me full circle."

"Is she honest about her evil ways? All women have them, but to really understand them, she must first embrace them. The mind of a woman is more dangerous than anything you can think of."

"We are working on that."

"It's an energy that draws women to you, nothing more. She sees potential. Just take your time, and respect her realness. It's hard for women to bear their souls. But when they do, you have to mold them. Women are a reflection of their men."

"You talk like a man of experience," Moon said, trying to read Rayven.

"Nah, lil' homie. It's just that I understand women a little better because I'm a little bit older than you. For real, I wish I could have any one of these bitches around here."

"If you could fuck just one chick in here, who would it be?"

"Shid! Probably Hopkins," Rayven said.

"Yeah, I like Hopkins, too, but she acts like a bitch sometimes."

"Yeah, she does." Rayven knew Moon was right.

Chapter 3

Buttons had been going through shit over the past couple of days. Her mind was playing tricks on her. She couldn't figure out if she was raped or if she, in fact, gave Ralph the pussy. The mental pain was worse than any physical pain she had endured. Buttons was trying to remember if Nichelle had set her up.

Oh my God, all three of them. Over and again. I'm a fucking freak. I ain't worth shit. I'm really a slut. Buttons couldn't get the images out of her head.

Buttons had been ducking Nichelle for about two days, afraid to face her. She didn't know what she was going to do. She needed someone to talk to. The only thing she knew for sure was, somehow, she would get revenge. She couldn't bring herself to call the police, not because she didn't want to, but because she just didn't want her name and history all over the news. Also, she knew Ralph would be spared if she snitched. Nobody protected a snitch in the hood, at the end of the day.

What had her fucked up the most was the fact that she somehow enjoyed the fact that she'd fucked Nichelle's man. *That bitch was always running around with Keisha, bragging about having the best pussy on earth. Look at her man. though, chasing this white pussy.* Buttons was confused, her young mind unable to see the bigger picture.

"Hello," Buttons said once she heard someone pick up the phone on the other end of the line.

"Yeah… What's up, girl? No… I've just been laying low... I don't know… I got to go school shopping with my mother today… Damn! When did that happen? So they don't know who shot him? That's fucked up." Buttons was having a conversation with Keisha. She wanted to tell Keisha about the shit that happened at Nichelle's house, but she couldn't get it out. Buttons felt like Yusra might be the only one she could talk to anyway.

"So you had fun, huh? I know that's right… I wish I would have gone with you… No reason. It's just that I know Dewey can fuck. I remember that time he was fucking you while me and Curtis were fucking right next to y'all… Yeah, that was the same night the bitch came through the window." Buttons laughed as she reminisced. "That bitch was crazy. She tried to kill you over that dick. I wonder if that's the girl he's still fucking with?"

Buttons got off the phone with Keisha, and Nichelle called, but Buttons didn't have any rap and got right off the phone. In her heart, she somehow knew that Nichelle was to blame for what happened at her house. *So what if I enjoyed it? I'm still going to get that shady bitch back!*

Knock, knock.

"Who is it?" Buttons yelled toward the door.

"Leroy."

"Open the door," she ordered, rolling over on the bed.

"Look. Your mother said you needed some school clothes and shit," Leroy said, stepping into the room.

"Yeah, I do," Buttons said, knowing he was going to make her work for it, which was cool with her. It was ammo for her gun of revenge. Everybody was going to pay one day.

"Well, come over here and earn it." Leroy pushed his sweatpants down to his knees so that his dick was free. He didn't have any underwear on.

"You're a fucking pervert," Buttons said and meant it, but she still climbed off the bed and went to her knees to earn her school clothes.

"I know," Leroy spoke as he grabbed her head. "I also know how bad you want those school clothes."

* * * * *

"What are you reading?" Moon asked.

"I don't read; I study. So, I'm studying 'The Unseen Hand', by A. Ralph Epperson. It's an introduction to the conspiratorial view of history," Rayven answered.

"Not that conspiracy theory shit again." Moon shook his head. "That's why you're crazy now."

Laughing, Rayven said, "My evidence is all around here, so we'll see who's crazy in the end. What you got your hands on?"

"It's an anthology by a few of my favorite authors. It's called 'Tradin' War Stories'. This joint is wicked," Moon said. "The nephews in the Atlanta story. This that gangsta shit! It's about standing on business no matter what."

"Respect. You can learn from anything, but this here"—Rayven held up the book that he was studying—"this is about them real gangsters."

"Shiddd, we're the real gangsters. We're the niggas that them rappers be rapping about."

"That's what they want you to believe. We aren't even close to being real gangstas. Yeah, we did some gangsta shit. We stood up while others folded, but we still ended up broke and locked up for life, and for what? One, two bodies? What's gangsta about that?" Rayven asked.

"I stood tall and carried my own weight when a nigga tried me," Moon fired proudly.

"Okay, and you still broke," Rayven said. "These motherfuckers use wars to obtain and hold power. How do you think that the younger and more dangerous are kept under control?"

"Fear."

"Exactly. Fear. Chaos always brings order, and the threat of war preserves power, whereas a warning only serves to protect people from danger."

"Okay, what about the niggas that don't fear nothing or care about any of that shit?"

"Any man that doesn't fear nothing is a damn fool, and they're killed off, but listen, man. They got gangs for people who think they can win."

"What, like the Bloods and Crips? The BGF and shit?"

"Fuck no! Gangs have been around since the beginning of time. I'm talking about the Masons, the Catholic Church, Capitalism, and Communism. They are the real gangs. Do you know who the Rothschild and Rockefeller families are?"

"Not the Rothschilds, but the Rockefellers are the people Jay Z named his company after, right?"

"True, but it's deeper than that. These two families were involved in everything. They were the two heads of power back in the day. They still have their hands in everything, even today, but everything that happens is about controlling the four centers of power."

"Centers of power?"

"Yeah."

"What the fuck is that?"

"Money, intelligence, Christians, and government. The whole world is run by secret societies. These people start wars, drop atomic bombs that kill millions, and bring drugs straight from Red China."

"Who are these people?"

"The controllers of this country. The puppet-masters. The hidden hands. They are the motherfuckers who keep their foot on the backs of all black, Mexican, and poor white people. They are the ones who force you to write African American on your application instead of American, even though you can't be American. Do you know how many people would have jobs and enter schools of higher education if they were able to just put American as a race?"

"So it's all a setup?"

"Yeah. We, as poor people, are born enemies of the government. Our only crime is being black and poor."

"What about Castro and Bin Laden? America out to get them too? Them two crazy motherfuckers tried to kill us."

"Did you just say *us*?"

"Yeah. My family could have been in the wrong place at the wrong time. I might kill them niggas if I see them."

"You got a lot to learn, Moon, but I got you. Let me learn you something. Castro and Bin Laden were both created by the American government. They rebelled once they realized what they were trained to do. Any real man with a heart will rebel against the evil devils who run this country once they get a true look at the system of things. The media makes people like the Black Panthers, Malcolm X, Castro, Minister Louis Farrakhan, and the Nation of Islam out to be heartless, when the truth is, this country is heartless—"

"I fuck with the Panthers. I didn't like how they treated the women in the party, but I respect what they were about. Malcolm X was my man too," Moon cut Rayven off.

"Listen. Like I was saying, they order the deaths of millions of innocent women and children. They flood our communities with all kinds of drugs that they create, then lock us up and take the money we make from the drugs. They trade information for drugs with China and other countries alike. Nothing happens that they don't know about. September 11th, Pearl Harbor, World Wars I and II—it's all planned. They want a one-world government. That's what the U.N. is, and for the record, don't ever let someone tell you who your enemies are. Only a fool does that. Make your own enemies. These people create the conditions that bring about the crimes, then use the crime to justify the conditions. Trust me. It's another level of evil."

"I feel that shit because we ain't bringing that shit over here, and we don't make guns. Plus, I don't let nobody tell me who my enemies are."

"You just did. America said 'we' were at war with Bin Laden and them, and you got right with it. They're not your enemy. Truthfully, they are soldiers of the same struggle. We all want freedom, be it worldly or heavenly."

"Okay, I can respect that, being as though you broke it down, but if all that other shit is true, then why did Castro and them become outcasts?"

"You can't beat the runners of this country if you're still attached to this country. This is how Castro and Bin Laden are able to survive. I got some shit for you to read. You want to learn who the real gangsters are?"

"Yeah, let me check some of that shit out," Moon said, needing to see and read it himself. Rayven loved the fact that Moon wouldn't let somebody tell him anything.

"I got you. I'ma make you the unseen hand." Rayven laughed.

"I'm already the unseen hand," Moon assured him. And Rayven knew that he was telling the truth.

"Mr. Lewis, are you coming out to clean the dayroom up?" Ms. Hopkins popped up at the door, and you could see 85 percent of her face in the door window.

"Yeah. Are you ready now?"

"Nah. After I finish doing my count," she said, then continued to make the 10 a.m. count.

"Damn," Moon said and jumped up when the second officer helping with the count passed their door.

"That's Taylor little chocolate ass. Shorty little fine ass is phat to death."

"Yeah, she is thick. She got a baby by that dude Fair, right?" Rayven spoke, but his mind was uptown.

"Yeah. That nigga can't handle that pussy. I know he can't. I would blaze her little sexy chocolate ass. I would be all up in that joint."

"Would you eat it?"

"Hell yeah!" Moon said as if it went without saying.

"You some nasty little motherfuckers."

"I know you ate pussy before."

"Nah, that wasn't the thing in my day."

"You need to try it. Maybe you wouldn't have so many women problems."

In prison, every nigga thought he had the best game. The debates were always about women—hood and Hollywood bitches alike. On the other hand, niggas were beefing about whose rap game was the best. Niggas would fight about their favorite rappers as if they gave a fuck about any of them. The questions were, "Why is he fucking with her? Do you think she's a freak for real?" etcetera.

Rayven tried not to get into that. He tried to focus on getting home because if he spent all his time like the other prisoners, worrying about what somebody else was doing, he wouldn't go anywhere in life. Shit! How could he? Instead of working on himself and doing shit for himself, he would be putting all his time and energy into worrying about what other people were doing. So what if a rich nigga had an ugly woman? Let him do him! When love was the source of a relationship, neither money nor looks could be involved.

"Let me put this gun (toothbrush) in my mouth so I can go out here and clean up this fucking dayroom," Rayven said, talking to himself.

"Damn, dug, you reading all that rebel shit, and you around here cleaning up and shit?" Moon called Rayven on his job.

"Yeah, baby boy. I needs that thirty dollars a month."

"Okay, Lewis! You got one hour to clean up and hit the shower!" Officer Hopkins yelled down the tier as their cell door opened just as Rayven finished spitting toothpaste in the toilet bowl.

"Okay. That's your call, Mr. Clean," Moon said, laughing.

"You got jokes?"

"Aye, Yo, where are the books at?" Moon asked, referring to the hardcore 'Black Video Illustrated' and the Buttman Magazines that they kept in the cell. Moon knew that Rayven was going to be gone for at least an hour, so he was going to take a good shit and beat his dick real quick.

"Under the bunk. All of them are in that big box by the wall," Rayven responded. He had about fifteen girl books and ten freak novels that dudes had given to him.

"Good looking, Jeffery," Moon joked, laughing hard as shit as Rayven left the cell.

* * * * *

Buttons was in the bathroom, spitting up and gagging. She had just swallowed over twenty pain pills. *What the fuck is wrong with you? It ain't that bad. You in this bitch trying to kill yourself. For what? Because of some weak motherfucker? Nah, fuck that!* After Buttons had sucked her stepfather's dick and eaten his cum, she rushed to the bathroom and tried to kill herself. Somewhere between life and death, she realized that killing herself was letting her foes win.

Nah, fuck that! You bitches going to have to kill me. I ain't going out without a fight.

Buttons looked in the mirror and decided right there that she had a whole lot to live for. *I'm going to put all my energy into school, but somebody will pay.*

Buttons went school shopping. She bought some open-toe shoes and two pairs of tennis with two hundred of the five hundred dollars Leroy had given her. She spent a ball (a hundred dollars) on a few shirts and jeans. She hit the ten-dollar shoe store with her last two hundred and got clothes and underwear. She knew she could mix it up with all the gear she already had. She was good. Everybody knew that the first two weeks of school were like a fashion show, with everybody wanting to see who would run out of fresh shit first.

"What's up, bitch?" Keisha questioned when she bumped right into Buttons coming out of the ten-dollar store in Westside Shopping Center.

"You know what it is, bitch."

"The mix!" they said in unison, referring to mixing name-brand clothes with off-brand shit. You had to be nice to pull it off.

"Shit, you might as well come back in with me," Keisha said.

Buttons and Keisha went back in the store and shopped like crazy. Keisha had a lot of cash on her. k

"Damn, bitch! Where you get all that cheese (money) from?" Buttons asked, then took a wild guess. She had clipped Dewey for his paper. *That's my bitch!*

"I found my brother's stash."

"Girl, is you crazy? Knocky gonna fuck you up."

"Fuck that nigga! He only gave me a little bit of money for school shopping anyway. Plus, I'm putting my shit over your house. He ain't going to know I got him. He's gonna think that my mother got him again."

Buttons knew Keisha's school clothes had been stolen from her house last year.

"So what now?" Buttons asked.

"Let's hit West View Mall. You know I got to treat my feet."

"Damn! What about your sister?" Buttons asked, trying to get something out of the deal too. Shit, she was the one keeping the shit.

"I got you, white girl. Just be cool, Snowflake," Keisha said, laughing and walking to the counter. "I would like to get my school discount." Keisha pulled out her school ID.

After Keisha paid for the shit she had, they walked over to the Supermarket and got a Lyft.

They stopped at Buttons' first to drop off the shit they had already before heading for West View Mall.

* * * * *

"Ooh, baby. Damn! Rayven. Ooh, Rayven, baby. Right there!" Correctional Officer Dhaka Hopkins was moaning as her back was pressed up against the wall inside the dayroom closet. Rayven was holding her up in the air while laying pipe. Their relationship had been going on for about five weeks now, almost since Dhaka had started working.

"Damn, baby! Ah, shit," Rayven was saying as he continued to keep Dhaka airborne. Dhaka had the best pussy he had ever had in his life. *Damn! This shit is good.* He didn't know if it was the fact that he was locked up that made it extra good, or the fact that her shit was always tight and wet. Dhaka's pussy never had a smell to it, and Rayven had no problem eating it. Her shit smelled like a variety of fruits.

"Don't move, baby. Don't move. Keep that shit right there! You better not move. Damn! Ooh, baby, right there," Hopkins said, rotating her hips in a circular motion. "Mmh, mmmhh. Fuck!"

Rayven was in a world of his own. He was in the softest place on earth. Babies lived there, and grown ass men tried their best to get back in there. There was nothing like the body of a woman. The mind and body of a woman were unexplainable. God knew what he was doing when he gave Eve to Adam. Rayven's knees started getting weak as he felt his soldiers marching forward.

"Aaarrrgh! Ah. Ooohh. You big, country dick nigga. I'm cumming, baby. I'm…" Dhaka loved older men. Rayven was her childhood crush. "Mmmhh…"

Rayven and Hopkins had another officer looking out for them. Rayven knew, more than likely, if someone snitched, it would be another prisoner. Dudes in prison were suckers like that. They always hated on real men

"I'm cumming too," Rayven said. He wasn't pulling out until she got hers. He kissed her in the mouth to keep down her moans. Dhaka tended to get loud when she was cumming. He slowed down to a very slow, steady stroke.

"Oooooh! Why are you slowing down, Rayven? Oh, baby! Damn! Dig me out. Punish this pussy! That's it!" Dhaka screamed into his mouth. "I'm there! I'm cumming, baby! Oooh!"

Rayven waited until she got hers, then pulled out and let Hopkins jerk him off until he nutted on the closet floor. Hopkins locked on to his shit real tight, pulling it strong but slow, biting her bottom lip and moaning as she watched his dick like a hawk. Rayven knew that she was cumming again when she locked onto him. Before he had gotten a cell buddy, she used to come to his door and get him to jerk off for her. He wasn't into that, but Dhaka called his cell the "Candy Shop". Her favorite line was "after you work up and sweat, you can play with the stick," referring to him doing his job before getting to nut. She got off on seeing him cum.

What made Dhaka go for Rayven, besides the fact that his tongue game was like no other, was the fact that he was so different, and he never changed his routine to get her attention like so many others. Dhaka knew that a man would always do him, but a lame would change up. She never trusted niggas who would do anything for attention. The fact that Rayven wasn't sweating her like the other lames only added to his swagger.

Some dudes would disrespect her by pulling out their little ass dicks. Most of the tickets (infractions) she wrote were because some nigga disrespected her by pulling out his penis. Once she found out that Rayven was the same Rayven who used to run with her father, the one that she had a crazy crush on as a child, that was it. The rest was history.

"You good?" Rayven asked once he put Dhaka down. He just looked at her sexy ass. *Damn, she bad,* he thought. *I got to get the fuck up town.*

"Yeah, I'm real good now," Dhaka replied with a big ass smile on her face while fixing her uniform.

"Well, go ahead out. I'll be out in a few minutes."

"I'm crazy about you. You do know that, right? I remember what the news said about you," Hopkins replied, stepping up and pulling Rayven down to kiss her. "Here."

"You know you're my baby. And I told you before that the news don't report 'news'. It creates it." Rayven watched as she pulled out something wrapped in plastic. "What's this?"

"Just take it. I love real niggas, and you're one of them."

Rayven waited until Hopkins was gone before he looked into the plastic. It was some weed. He smiled.

That young girl is going to be the death of an old man if I keep fucking her back-to-back like this. I'm not as young as I used to be. Rayven had to sit down for a minute to get some energy.

"Alright, Lewis! You got five minutes!" Hopkins yelled up to him in the shower.

"Yes, ma'am." Rayven laughed. "I'm on my way out now." Rayven admired her style.

"Well, you need to put a move on it. Don't get yourself a ticket," Hopkins warned.

"Ayo, Rayven, fuck that bitch!" someone yelled out the side of one of the cell doors.

"Ayo, Ms. Hopkins! Suck my dick, bitch!" another inmate fired from an unknown cell.

"Yeah. Fuck that dick-eating ass bitch!" another added.

"Your mother," Hopkins fired back. She enjoyed getting the young inmates fired up. It made her eight hours pass more quickly. Many of the female officers viewed the prisoners as a joke. They would let you talk any kind of way just to kick their eight hours. Dudes would be running around, talking about how much a female does for him, but trust, if it was that serious, a nigga would know it. To be honest, Hopkins viewed most inmates as clowns. All her co-workers did. Their entire lunch breaks were about who was the biggest clown in the institution.

"Bitch, you crazy? A nigga will crush you." And from there, it was on. They would curse her out for the rest of her shift. She would just sit at her desk and listen to them call her all kinds of names. Some officers seemed to need the abuse. Some of them even craved it. If a nigga didn't say shit to them all day, they would start doing dumb shit. Nobody wanted to be ignored.

"You need to stop, Ms. Hopkins," Rayven mumbled, coming down the steps from the top shower in case someone could hear him. He knew what she was up to, like he knew the walls had ears. He had told her not to play with these kids before. They had too much time to be fucking with. He never told her not to do her job, but going out of the way to fuck with people would buy her that knife. Rayven knew that if she got hit by a convict, there was nothing he could do. He wasn't jumping out there for no C.O. It didn't matter who she was or how good the pussy was.

"Man, shorty be tripping on you," Moon said once Rayven stepped in, and the cell door closed.

"Yeah, it's cool."

"She gon' make a nigga go upside her head," Moon said as he peeped at her from the side of the door.

"I'm about to lay down." Rayven started putting on his deodorant.

"Man, you really are getting old. That job be knocking your old ass out."

"I like to see you try putting in the work I do when you get my age. I work out in the morning and then have to clean the whole dayroom."

"Man, that ain't shit."

"Yeah? Well, why aren't you in tip-top shape, young nigga? Look at my shit," Rayven said, showing off his rock-hard seven-and-a-half-pack and big chest.

"All those muscles don't mean shit no more. You've been locked up too long. This is that bedroom look," Moon said, showing his chest and gut. "That's old school. This is that new shit."

"Nigga, don't no woman want that shit. You're too young to be busted up like that." Rayven was laughing. "That new shit you're talking about is bullshit."

"It's about that money now, playboy."

"Yeah, with them hood rats. A woman should be the only thing soft in a relationship. How are you and your girl gonna have a big stomach?"

"Man, I ain't listening to that shit. Where your girl at, nigga? Niggas with no girls are worse than a woman with no man. They always have the best advice on how to keep a man but ain't never got none."

"That was my problem. I had a girl when, truth be told, I've always needed a woman."

"How old were your folks?"

"Age doesn't make a woman. A woman ain't what she wears, how old she is, or how many niggas she's fucked. A woman is what she knows—her strengths, her weaknesses, and her struggles."

"Yeah, okay, Doctor Phil," Moon said.

"So what's a freak?"

"A bitch fucking a lot of niggas."

"No. A freak is a female who is supposed to be with one dude but fucks around on him. A freak is not a chick that fucks a lot of dudes when she's not in a relationship. She just likes to fuck. If a chick fuck with me for a month, you for two months, and him for three months, as long as she fucks with only us, one at a time, she's not a freak. She just hasn't found what she's looking for yet."

"Yeah, whatever. Now you're Captain Save-a-Hoe. First Mr. Clean, now Captain Kirk."

"I'm gone on that note," Rayven said and lay back on the bed and waited for sleep to come. Rayven felt good for the moment. He wanted to get in a quick nap before lunch.

Another day in the penitentiary. Rayven thought, closing his eyes.

* * * * *

"It's still early. We might as well go see a movie," Keisha suggested. They had already bought a couple of pairs of tennis shoes.

"Cool. You must got more money than you're telling me about."

They went to the movies and saw a movie that neither one of them would remember. After the movie, they went and got something to eat. Then they went to get on the bus that would take them back to the city

"Keisha," Buttons said, then paused. "I don't trust that bitch, Nichelle."

"Why? What's up?" Keisha questioned.

"It's just something about her. She always wants us to pop E-pills and shit. I think that bitch trying to tum us out."

"Did that bitch try something?" Keisha asked, sitting up in her seat. They were on the bus, Buttons on the window side. "We can fuck that bitch up."

"Nah. She ain't do nothing. It's just that I don't trust her."

"Alright, girl. I'll watch that bitch. But you know you are my sister, and if that bitch jumps out there, I'll fuck her up." Keisha was always ready to fight for Yusra or Buttons.

"I know."

"Well, we both already know that she's a shady bitch! Look at how she be carrying LunchMeet, and he took care of that bitch. Now he's locked up, and that bitch doesn't show him no love for real. His mother be having to chase her around and shit."

"You're right about that. But she claims to love him. What part of love is that? If a nigga treated me like he treated her when he was home, I would at least hold him down as a friend."

"What's crazy is that LunchMeet doesn't even ask for shit. And he still be looking out for her. I saw that bitch ignore his calls and all that shit. I say all that to say, if she ain't real with that nigga, you know she's a backstabbing bitch."

Buttons started laughing, knowing that Keisha was dead serious. They would never cross each other. If one started fighting and wasn't winning, the other jumped in, and they both rumbled.

"Your stepfather is a nasty somebody!" Keisha laughed walking back into Buttons' bedroom after using the bathroom.

"What did he do?" Buttons inquired.

"This old ass nigga walked in the bathroom while I was using it, talking about he was sorry. This nigga tried to get a free peep at this pussy," Keisha said, laughing. "I told that nigga that he would have to pay the next time."

"Girl, you crazy." Buttons shook her head. She knew that Leroy would get himself fucked up, playing with Keisha.

"I'm for real. I told him that if he ever did that shit again, I would get my brother to stomp a mud hole in his chump ass."

Knock, knock.

"Open the door, Leroy." Buttons knew it was him.

"Keisha, again, I'm sorry. I really made an honest mistake." Leroy sounded scared as shit. Everybody knew Keisha's brother was robbing and killing everything and would fuck something up about his baby sister.

"Yeah, whatever, nigga. Just don't let that shit happen again," Keisha warned, laughing at the sucker inside.

"You got it," Leroy said and walked out.

As soon as the door closed, Buttons and Keisha burst out laughing. Buttons had never seen anybody handle Leroy like that. She was thinking of saying that she was Knocky's girl. That way, Leroy would leave her alone unless she wanted him to fuck with her.

"Put that new shit about the city on,"" Keisha directed lying across the bed.

"You talking about that series the girl NeNe and Delmont put out?"

"Yeah, what's the name of that shit?" j

"Bodymore, Murderland, or something like that."

"Yeah, that's it. Murderland," Keisha remembered. "That shit serious. And I fucks with that nigga Billy Lo."

"Girl, fuck Billy Lo," Buttons fired. "I be wondering if that bitch Snoop can really eat pussy."

"Bitch, bye! You know you ain't letting another bitch eat that pussy. And you better not let Yusra hear you talking about Snoop; that's her baby!"

They watched season one of *Murderland* until they passed out on Buttons' bed. Jessica came in and turned off the flat screen TV.

* * * * *

After the shift change, Rayven went out to the dayroom for a minute. When the officer called for gym, he went to the barbershop to get his haircut. His barber had just finished cutting someone's hair, so he got right in the chair.

"... Man, Nas is tight. But who's fucking with Jay? Nobody." Yeyo, the barber, was talking shit. Jay Z was his number one rapper. "And y'all better respect Biggie."

"Nigga, is you crazy, dumb, or high? Jay is cool, I give you that. His rap game is on another level. And Biggie shit is wicked, too, but let's keep it real. Neither one of them are fucking with Tupac," another older barber name Smokey added his two cents. "I fucks with Beanie Siegel too."

"Rayven, tell these nigga's something," Yeyo said, looking down at him as he started cutting him a bald head.

"I don't fuck with none of them. Nas cool. I fucked with that Ether and One Mic joint, but on the real, all them niggas be dry snitching," Rayven said.

Everybody looked at Rayven like he was crazy, but nobody challenged him. Yeyo knew he was set in his ways and always had some kind of crazy argument to back up his statements. Yeyo didn't feel like fucking with Rayven, so he just continued to cut his hair.

"Dry snitching?" someone was dumb enough to ask.

"Yeah, dry snitching. They all rap about shit that we still do. That's why I listen to Rock 'n' Roll."

"They don't talk about shit that I do. But that's what rap is." The nigga crazy enough to jump out there was a half-slick old head from Sandtown named Ernie Perny.

"What are you locked up for?"

"Drug trafficking," Ernie Perny said.

"Point proven. Your favorite rapper be talking about how and where to get work., how to move work, and all that other shit."

"You just crazy," Ernie Perny said before getting up and rolling out. Everybody knew that he was right, but Rayven did have a point. Yeyo and Smokey went back and forth about the latest.

"Good looking out, Yeyo. I got you," Rayven said, getting out of the barber's chair to shake off the loose hair. "Let me holler at you for a minute, Yeyo."

"What's up, Rayven?" Yeyo asked once they were in the hallway.

"Yo, I got some weed, so if anybody is looking, send them to me. Plus, tell Driver I got something for him."

"A'ight, but let me get some of that shit too. I'll put you in the book for free cuts," Yeyo said, trying to get his. Everybody in prison had a line.

"Here," Rayven said, giving him what he had already planned to give him anyway. "You ain't got to do that. You know I fuck with y'all like that." Rayven was referring to Yeyo and his two co-defendants, Clayton and Driver.

As soon as they got back to the barbershop, they saw correctional officers running down the compound toward a code. About two to three minutes later, they saw the medical people running with someone on the stretcher. Next came the officers walking Ernie Perny and another bleeding nigga up the compound in handcuffs.

Damn! I know I ain't make shorty that mad. Rayven was watching the police go crazy out there.

"Smokey, I think the police just got hit," another barber said.

"Well, that will get us locked down for a minute," Smokey said.

The warden didn't care about prisoners stabbing each other, but once his officers started getting hit, he was going to lock the joint down and fuck some shit up, looking for weapons, drugs, and cell phones.

"Okay, gentlemen, go back to your buildings," the officer ordered, stepping into the barbershop.

"Ayoo, Ms. Mann, what happened?" Rayven asked. Mann was a cool, slim, dark-chocolate female officer with a tight body.

"Somebody was getting stabbed, and a dumb ass officer jumped in the way of the knife and got stabbed. That's why we get issued mace," she said. Mann was another officer Rayven wouldn't mind fucking. "They don't pay me enough."

"I heard that." Rayven nodded in understanding before walking off. With the information he had just gotten, it was a toss-up if they would get locked down and shook down just because the police got hit.

Chapter 4

It was mid-September, and school was in full swing. Buttons and Keisha attended Southwestern High School and were in the twelfth grade. Keisha had failed the ninth grade. However, they were in different classes.

"Girl, I can't stand my first-period teacher! He is drilling us to death. I mean, damn! School just started," Keisha stressed to Buttons as they made their way through the school doors after hearing the bells. It was their second week of school.

"Cut his class," Buttons responded. She was carrying her books in her hand.

"I can't. Girl, he's crazy about roll call."

"My teacher is cool." Buttons loved school, but she still couldn't wait to finish.

Buttons and Keisha were dressed in mini-skirts, heels, and tight, body-hugging shirts, as always.

"Well, look. I will see you at lunch time, girl," Keisha said as they walked up to her homeroom class.

Just as she spoke, four chicks walked past. The hallway was crowded with ninth, tenth, eleventh, and twelfth graders trying to make it to homeroom. One of the girls who attended the same class as Keisha bumped Buttons.

"Watch where you're going, bitch!" Buttons barked, rolling her eyes and neck long, slow, and hard. She knew the hallway wasn't that crowded when she realized who it was.

"What?"

"You heard her, bitch!" Keisha added for clarity.

"And what?"

Keisha and Buttons took a step forward. Keisha and Buttons knew the girls ran from Westside Shopping Center to Mount Street. They were known as the Four Horsemen, a clique of four bitches that were known for fighting and leaning on bitches. The Lucky Charms and the Four Horsemen fought once when they jumped Yusra. Buttons dropped her books. For a white girl, she could rumble. Shit, she grew up on the Avenue.

"Fuck these freak bitches!" one of the four said.

"You wish," Buttons fired back.

"Bitch! I wouldn't fuck you if I had a dick. All the Westside niggas that had that loose pussy said your pussy smell like a creek," the littlest of the crew fired, and they all laughed.

"And still, your boyfriend ate it."

"Bitch!" The littlest one got in Buttons' face. "What's up, white girl?" She pushed Buttons, and Keisha swung but didn't connect.

"Aye, ladies, what's going on here?" the school support staff member asked, breaking through the now gathering crowd. "I said, what's going on?" He looked around, but nobody answered. He looked at the girls. "Let's move."

Everybody started moving. The girls kept their eyes on each other. Keisha mouthed the words, "Eat this pussy bitch!" after one of the girls flipped them the middle finger.

"I will see you later," Buttons said, hugging Keisha.

"Okay." Keisha was still ready to go. "Watch yourself."

"I will cut me a bitch."

"I know that's right."

"What's up, girl?" Buttons asked as she took her seat next to Nova. Buttons was still a little edgy.

Buttons had met Nova and her homegirl Janette on the first day of school. They were all in the same first three classes. Buttons found both to be cool as shit. They were her classroom buddies.

"Ain't shit, girl. Did you see Janette out there?"

"Nah. I almost got into it with the Four Whoremen." Buttons started laughing at the inside joke.

"Irina and them?" Nova asked in between laughing.

"Mmmhmm."

"You better watch those bitches. They be stabbing bitches and shit."

"Fuck them hoes. We already rolled around with them bitches. They know how the Charms get down."

"Okay, class. The bell has rung, so it's my time now," Ms. White, the twelfth-grade teacher, said, standing at the front of the class. "Let's quiet down so I can do roll call."

Ms. White waited for a few seconds for the classroom talk to settle down. Ms. White was a heavy-set, brown-skinned sister who had taught fifth grade up until 2013 when her best friend and girlfriend, Ms. Childs, another teacher, retired.

"Okay. Tucker—Darby—Byers—Ralston—…" Ms. White was checking off names as kids yelled or said *here* or *present* when their name was called. "—Howard—"

"Here," Buttons said.

"Ray… Ray…" Ms. White repeated when no one answered. "Spirit—"

"Here," Nova responded, hoping Janette would come on.

"Lance—Witherspoon—Matthews…" Ms. White finished the roll call after calling about five more names. She knew her class was overcrowded, but what could she do? She was truly one of the few teachers who really cared.

"May I help you?" Ms. White asked when a young girl entered the classroom.

Everybody turned around to see Janette standing at the front of the classroom. Ms. White's desk was behind everybody so she could keep a watchful eye on her entire class. The entrance of the classroom was through the front and exited through the back, which was where her desk sat.

"Sorry I'm late," Janette said, feeling dumb. There was nothing worse than being late because everybody watched extra hard. It was a good thing Janette was dressed to impress.

"I take it that you are Ms. Gramly?"

"Yes, ma'am."

"Have a seat, Ms. Gramly. You owe me twenty minutes after school. Okay, class, continue." Ms. White sat back down.

Damn, Janette! Buttons looked at her girl and saw that she wasn't feeling that detention shit.

"She's a crazy bitch!" Nova whispered. "She knows how homeroom is."

"She must not." Buttons tried to whisper but couldn't.

"Gramly and Howard, I will be looking at your drills in two minutes," Ms. White said.

It amazed Buttons how Ms. White knew that it was her and Janette whispering, let alone remembering their names. "I ain't finished." Buttons was rushing to finish.

"You must be if you're talking."

Buttons was now focused on the ten drill questions. *Think, girl.* She was stuck on the fifth problem. *Skip it, Buttons,* she thought to herself. Her mind was racing. Buttons hated to fail at anything. That was one of the good traits she had gotten from her mother.

"Time is up. Bring me the drills."

Buttons got up to hand in her drill. "Here's mine," she said, handing Ms. White the drill.

"And Ms. Howard," Ms. White spoke as Buttons was walking away.

"Yes?" Buttons stopped and halfway laced her.

"The next time you feel like talking, don't do it on my time."

"Yes, ma'am," Buttons replied seconds before the homeroom bell rang.

"You good?" Keisha questioned, walking up on Buttons as she exited her classroom.

"Yeah," Buttons assured. "My teacher just blew me."

"Where are them Four Horsemen bitches?" Keisha questioned, ignoring Buttons' statement.

"Them bitches don't want no smoke. They're not crazy," Buttons spoke loud enough to be heard.

"I know that. I just likes to keep an eye on them bitches, especially the little one I don't like. Bitch thinks that she is all that. I'ma fuck that bitch's man, watch." Keisha rolled her eyes.

"That's my girl." Buttons high-fived her.

Buttons and Keisha were sitting in the jammed-packed cafeteria, eating slices of pizza from the hot bar. Keisha also had her chocolate milk and butter crunch cookies, which always made Buttons sick to her stomach. She was cool with her Diet Coke and chips.

"How do you eat that? You eat like you're pregnant." Buttons looked on as Keisha continued to dip the cookies into the milk. "Yuck."

"It's a black thing." Keisha laughed.

"Yeah, whatever! It seems like a hoe thing to me. Especially since all the bitches I see eating it are school sluts. N-E-way, what are we doing after school?"

"I don't know. I was thinking of going down the Avenue to see what's going on down there."

"Buttons!" Nova and Janette walked past, carrying their lunch trays, and spoke in unison.

"Hey!"

"Who was that?" Keisha questioned curiously, watching the two females disappear into the crowded cafeteria once they took a seat.

"Two bitches from homeroom."

"What's up with them?" Keisha was so overprotective of Buttons. "Where are they from?"

"I think Murphy Holmes, maybe even Philadelphia. I don't know." Buttons hunched her shoulders because she wasn't really suret. She thought she heard Janette bragging about Philadelphia, but she also talked about attending Brooker T. Washington. "They're both just cool as shit."

"We got to go down the Avenue to meet up with Nichelle and Yusra after school, now that I think about it," Keisha changed the subject. She was territorial when it came to her girls.

Buttons could sense Keisha's jealousy but kept it to herself. "Alright. Once we all get together, then we can figure out what to do."

"For real, I want to go downtown to Mula's."

"For what?" Buttons asked rhetorically because she knew that Keisha was referring to the strip club that Nichelle had turned them on to. Nichelle had a hookup with this big time, East Baltimore real-estate broker named Burgess who actually owned Mula's and would allow them to dance from time to time. As long as he got his cut and some slow neck every time. Buttons didn't like the deal, but she definitely needed the money. However, Keisha loved it. After all, she wasn't the one sucking dick, and they only had to give Nichelle 50 percent.

At the end of each night, they paid Nichelle, and she went upstairs to pay Burgess. They threw her a little extra since she was the one who put it all together. It had all begun been about three weeks just before school started. Buttons had only danced twice, but the extra cash was addictive.

The club was located in the heart of Downtown Inner Harbor, right on Baltimore Street, next door to Crazy John's, directly across the street from 'Rosie's, one of the most popular lounges in the city.

"What else?" Keisha started twerking right there for all to see. Everybody knew that she craved attention. "To dangle this pussy in them niggas' face so that I can get that money out of their pockets."

"I don't know," Buttons said. She was faking for real. She needed the cash, and she hated asking Leroy for money.

"Bitch, stop playing. You love that green too. Where else can you get so much money for so little? Get to see all kinds of dick, and you get paid for it in one place."

Bitch ain't lying! Buttons knew Keisha was speaking the truth. She'd gotten very turned on from dancing for guys, feeling their dicks poke at her thin thong. One guy had even pulled out and beat his shit right there in the open as she danced. Buttons was starting to believe that if not every black man, then most had big dicks when compared to white men. *She just wished that they all knew how to use them big motherfuckers.* "You're right about that."

"I know I am."

"I'm just scared of getting caught. Nichelle said that if we get locked up, we are on our own." Buttons was afraid to go to jail. She had heard stories about the Big Momma's House.

"As long as you don't trick in the club, you won't get locked up. They are not going to leave us locked up. Burgess just can't speak up, because he could lose his license. We're really too young to be stripping. They will make sure we're okay if anything happens. Plus, shid, you're one of the only three white girls who dance there, and you got them bitches beat," Keisha confessed, honestly. She still couldn't understand why all the niggas went crazy when Buttons got on the stage. It had to be because she was what they called a snow bunny.

"I know. I just be scared. I won't officially be eighteen until December."

"Yeah, two months before me." Keisha hated when people brought up her age, because, although she had a baby face, she had the body and build of a grown woman, so nobody questioned her.

The lunch bell rang and brought them back to school. "I will see you after school. Meet me by the front doors," Keisha said, getting up.

"Yes, mommy," Buttons joked, and Keisha rolled her eyes at the sarcasm and headed to class.

“Over here, Keisha!” Buttons called over the loud crowd of kids flooding the front of the school when she spotted her. “Keisha!”

Looking around after hearing Buttons call her name, Keisha peeped Buttons coming through the crowd. “Damn, bitch. You stick out like a sore thumb. I couldn’t miss you,” Keisha said as they came up and hugged each other. “I was just here, and l ain’t see you.”

“Some dude had me held up outside of last period with his weak rap game,” Buttons said then saw him coming. “Oh my God, girl, here he comes again.”

“Who?” Keisha was looking at the many faces in the coming crowd, some of whom didn’t even attend their school. “Which one?”

“The real black one right there.” Buttons tilted her head in his direction, hoping not to be seen.

“The tall one?”

“Yes, girl.”

“Damn, bitch!” Keisha looked at the tall, black nigga. “At least he’s fresh like he got some money.” She was trying to figure out if he was Jamaican or from out of town because he didn’t have Baltimore swagger. “Where that nigga from?” He passed them by then.

“I don’t know. His name is Montego, and guess what?”

“What?”

“He said he has a twin.” Buttons laughed at the thought.

“Damn!” was all Keisha could get out. She didn’t think it could get any worse. There was no way she could stomach two of them. “I hope they are not identical.”

“Don’t put your life on it. I will give him this. He has some nice poems that he wrote.” Buttons had listened to him read a few of his poems in her last period.

“At least he got something going for himself.” Keisha and Buttons busted out laughing.

“Make that two things.”

Keisha looked to see what Buttons was referring to.. "Damn, he might can get it." They watched as the African-looking nigga climbed into a new, black Lexus GS.

* * * * *

"It's about time," Nichelle said once Buttons and Keisha got within hearing range. "Time is money." Nichelle and Yusra were sitting on the Avenue on the hood of Nichelle's car by Harlem Park Middle School, which was around the corner from Buttons' house.

"What took y'all so long?" Yusra asked, arms crossed over her chest with a stand-off twist in her hips. She didn't like waiting for people when they were bullshitting around.

"Buttons got held up by her new man," Keisha spat.

Buttons shot her a look. "Don't even play like that," Buttons replied.

"Her new man?" Yusra questioned, looking from Keisha to Buttons.

"It's nothing." Buttons didn't feel like playing, so she quickly changed the subject. "So, what's good? Are we going to the club or what?"

Yusra looked at her like she had lost her damn mind. She hadn't waited for them to go to a club.

Dollar signs jumped in Nichelle's eyes. "Yes. Plus, it's gentlemen's night. All the ballers are going to be there." Nichelle wanted to go anyway. She just didn't want to be the one to bring it up first.

"Y'all need help. There is no way that I'm shaking my ass for a buck!" Yusra barked seriously.

Nichelle rolled her eyes. She hated when Yusra got on her righteous shit and acted like her shit didn't stink.

"Ain't nobody ask for your opinion, Yusra," Nichelle fired.

"Just like ain't nobody ask for yours," Yusra barked as her little-man complex kicked in.

Nichelle didn't respond.

After they apologized to Yusra and went back and forth for a minute, Yusra let it go. Still, she wasn't trying to hear shit Nichelle was saying. "Anyway, Buttons," Yusra cut Nichelle off as she tried to say sorry. "Let me holler at you for a minute." After they walked out of earshot, Yusra spoke again. "What are you doing?"

"What?"

"You know what. You don't need to dance at a club."

"I need the money, girl."

"Girl, please. Jessica takes good care of you. Don't be like Nichelle. That bitch is a freak with no morals, who is going nowhere in life. She doesn't want shit out of life. All she wants to do is fuck, club hop, and sit on the block."

Buttons knew that Yusra was right, to an extent. But Yusra didn't know her pain. Money wasn't free in her house. Shit, truth be told, it came easier at the club. "I just need to save up some money to move."

"So what? You're doing anything for money now? Just get a job."

"All we're going to do is dance, Yusra." Buttons took Yusra's statement as offensive.

"That's how they all start out. Then a month from now, you're in some backroom, getting your bottom knocked out. Look. I love you and Keisha like sisters. That bitch Nichelle is no good."

Buttons knew that Yusra was jive mad because she was cursing, and that was rare. "We will be okay."

"You're about to finish school. Don't start degrading yourself for no buck. I can understand Nichelle; that girl has no principles. That shit ain't for you and Keis. Just listen. It ain't worth it."

"Not everybody has a strong mother at home, Yusra." Buttons was jive emotional. She wished she had a mother like Yusra, a mother who loved her even when she failed and made mistakes, a mother's love that didn't change.

Yusra was a little caught off guard. She knew that loneliness was universal. People of all ages needed the security of being loved by someone important to them. Nobody wanted 'if' love. "I understand that, Buttons, but that's no reason to disgrace your mind and body." Yusra chose her words carefully. She didn't want to hurt her feelings. Yusra knew that she was blessed with one of the many unconditionally loving black mothers.

"Yusra, you're talking crazy. I told you that we aren't doing nothing but dancing," Buttons explained. People were always trying to stereotype something they didn't know shit about.

"What are you dancing for?" Yusra could respect the women dancing to accomplish something. It was women like Nichelle that she had no respect for. Buttons and Keisha didn't know any better, in her opinion, but women like Nichelle got into the clubs and did anything for a buck.

"I told you." Buttons was getting an attitude. Yusra didn't know what she had to endure at home with her mother, who loved some man more than her own child, a mother who hugged her only when she did something right and verbally abused her when she fucked up. "You just don't understand."

"Okay, girl. Just know that I love you, and you can come to me about anything." Yusra decided to let it drop. She didn't want to push Buttons away.

"I love you too."

"Buttons!" Nichelle called. "Are you coming, or are you going to stand here and listen to K-Love all day?" Nichelle made reference to a very popular and powerful, self-empowerment sister.

"Bitch…" Yusra just looked at Nichelle standing with her driver's side door open as if she was ready to go.

Keisha was already in the passenger seat.

"Look, Yusra. I have to go." Buttons started walking toward the car.

"Buttons, you don't have to go," Yusra said. She could see a little smirk on Nichelle's face. *Keep playing with fire, bitch!* Yusra thought.

"We will talk, girl. I promise." Buttons climbed into the back seat of the car behind Keisha. Yusra just stood there as Nichelle made an illegal U-turn and headed toward downtown.

"Yusra's little ass is crazy. She knows she wants some of this easy money," Nichelle said, pulling Buttons from her own thoughts.

Buttons desperately wanted to be loved, and to some extent, dancing in the club gave her that feeling and made her happy. It validated her to be wanted, even if it was only for sex. She just wanted to be loved and wanted. "Fuck Yusra. That bitch dick whipped right now," Buttons replied, but she felt something else. She felt like she had to get her money. *Fuck that.*

"I know that's right," Keisha said. "Let's go get this bag!"

They drove the rest of the way with light conversation.

* * * * *

They arrived at Mula's on foot, a little after five o'clock as a result of bullshitting. They got caught up in the rush-hour traffic. Nichelle had to park on one of the side streets of downtown.

"Where is Burgess?" Nichelle asked a chocolate stripper dressed in a red, open-nipple bra, a red G-string, and matching open-toe heels with twenties hanging from the red garter around her left leg.

There weren't a lot of customers in Mula's as of yet. It was still considered early in the strip world. Most of the seven to ten customers spread out throughout the club were either die-hard fans, stalkers, or just didn't want a lot of people to know they played the strip club scene.

"Where else?" The chocolate stripper replied, never stopping. She was trying to find her next victim.

"Y'all stay right here. As a matter of fact, have a seat. I'm going to see Burgess to see if we can get on the floor tonight." Nichelle knew he was upstairs in his office.

Buttons and Keisha watched the girls work their magic. The barmaid stayed busy. They talked as they sat in the corner of the club. It amazed them how easily the men would part with their hard-earned money in exchange for the thought of pleasure. It was truly a robbery by their own permission.

"Men are so fucking easy to control," Keisha said as she watched a nerdy-looking white boy creep into Mula's like someone was following him. She knew the hustlers didn't pour in until after ten. "All you have to do is tease them, and they will give you the world."

"You have to fuck their ego, girl," Buttons said, repeating something she'd heard her mother telling a friend.

"They think they really control everything, but truthfully, they don't. They work for us. It's a woman's world. They are just squirrels."

"Trying to get a what?" They both started laughing.

"Girl, you are crazy," Buttons said. She knew from her mother's relationship that 70 percent of the women in the world didn't truly understand their power over men. Leroy would never stray if her mother took care of business for real. Instead, he was able to control the relationship. Men were truly weak, they' were nothing without women. Everything they did, they did for women. Once a woman understood her power, she would never have another problem that she couldn't get a man to take care of.

Knock, knock.

"Come in."

Opening the door, Nichelle could see Burgess sitting behind his desk, counting money as she stepped into the room that doubled as an office.

"Nichelle!" Burgess smiled, always happy to see her.

"Hi, Burgess."

"What's up?" Burgess eye-fucked her. She could get his attention any time.

"Look. We're trying to dance tonight. Is that cool?"

"The pole is booked up, but you and your girls can work the tables as long as I get my 30 percent."

"Don't I always take care of you, big daddy?"."

"You do." Burgess grinned because he knew that Nichelle really took care of herself. She charged her girls 50 percent although it was only 30. But he didn't care just as long as he got his in more ways than one.

"Thanks, Burgess." Nichelle was headed for the door.

"And Nichelle." Burgess watched her fat ass shake.

Nichelle looked over her shoulder teasingly and spoke in a sexy tone. "Yes?"

"Be sure to bring the money up yourself," Burgess directed rubbing his dick under the table. It was something about that young girl's head that drove him crazy. It was just so sloppy and slow. And Nichelle had the softest throat he'd ever felt.

Nichelle didn't respond because she knew what time it was. Nothing was free on Baltimore Street. Everybody had something going on, so you were either paying or collecting. There was no in between.

"Let's go get dressed," Nichelle spoke, going to the table where Buttons and Keisha were sitting.

"What's your name, shorty?"

"Snow White," Buttons revealed. She was giving some light-skinned customer a lap dance. Her pussy was jive wet because she had done about six dances on the floor. Only Nichelle had gotten lucky enough to dance on the stage when one of the regular dancers didn't show up.

"You new, huh?" he asked, pushing his dick into her.

"Yeah." Buttons was trying to finish up. She couldn't wait for the song to end.

"I heard that." The clown bit his bottom lip and held on to Buttons' hips. "Damn! Go slow, Snow White. Yeah, just like that. Stay right there," he pleaded as he shook and nutted on himself right there in the club.

Another one had bit the dust. The club was full of no-good, nasty ass niggas. The girls in the club made bets to see who could make the most men nut on themselves. Buttons felt the slightly sticky wetness as it seeped through the clown's sweatpants. That kind of power always made Buttons smile inside. "You like that?"

"Hell yeah, I love it, but won't you let me get up in that white pussy for real? I got three hundred on me right now."

Buttons considered the offer for a moment. She could do a lot with three hundred dollars, but all money wasn't good money. Buttons finally spoke after a long pause. "No, thank you. I don't get down like that."

"Fuck you then, bitch!" The clown pushed Buttons out of his lap and stood up. "All y'all bitches the same! Get a nigga's dick all hard then play games," he fired, mad, before walking off, leaving Buttons standing there with her mouth hanging open. .

"What's up, bitch? Why are you standing here looking like Casper the Ghost?"

Buttons turned to find Keisha smiling. "That nigga just called me a bitch!"

It was cool for women to call each other bitches. Even men could get away with it if they were spending enough money or getting up in the pussy real good, but for some clown to just say it out of the blue was a no-no. It was like a white boy calling a black man 'nigga' out of the blue. Some could get away with it because they hung with black or grew up with blacks, but to scream it out of anger was an ass whipping.

"Who?" Keisha looked around.

"That clown right there." Buttons pointed the guy out like a star witness at a court hearing.

"Don't trip. I got him." Keisha's evil thoughts went into overdrive. "I got him. Go ahead and get your paper, girl. Fuck him."

"Okay." Buttons went off to put in some more lap dances.

"Get your fucking hands off me like that! You can't touch in here!" Keisha suddenly screamed.

Everybody in Mula's turned to see Keisha throwing her drink in some dude's face.

"Oh my God!" Buttons said when she realized it was the clown who'd called her a bitch.

"What, bitch? I didn't touch you!" the clowned argued, stepping aggressively toward Keisha.

He never made it. Two big ass bouncers got hold of him and, without asking questions, started punching and kicking him once he hit the floor. They beat him as they dragged him through the tables toward the back door. They liked fucking up a wild customer, but they loved beating a street thug. After all, they were off-duty cops.

"Oh. Yo, what the fuck!" The guy was trying to fight back. "Get the fuck up off me! Oh, bitch! Y'all done fucked up. You're gonna pay for this. I will be back," he threatened.

"Learn some respect for women. Just because we're dancers doesn't mean we're freaks!" Keisha screamed behind him. She looked over and winked at Buttons.

All the strippers and customers were clapping as Keisha screamed the truth. She looked so sincere.

The rest of the night was uneventful. Buttons walked away with $750, Keisha had five something, and Nichelle claimed to only have three., but everybody had witnessed her pick up more then that after her first set on stage.

At the end of the night, Buttons only pocketed a little over two hundred dollars after handing over 50 percent for Burgess and giving Nichelle her cut.

"Why do we always have to pay Nichelle? Shit, we already give Burgess half! Shit!" Keisha was venting to Buttons as they waited in the car for Nichelle.

"She is the one that got the hookup, so it's cool. Plus, she got the wheels and shit," Buttons defended, not really knowing why they had to pay her.

"I might step to that nigga Burgess myself. I don't trust that bitch." Keisha felt like they should see more of their money.

"Let's just wait until we see some evil."

"Well, I at least wish this bitch would come the fuck on. She does this shit every time it's time to go." Keisha was mad, and she wasn't feeling that they had to wait for Nichelle every time it was time to go, but she decided to trust Buttons' judgment.

"Yeah, you're right about that. I'ma say something to her ass about that too."

"We both are." Keisha fell into her own thoughts. "Got a bitch out here waiting on her dusty ass. She's probably in there fucking that greasy ass nigga. If I find out that that bitch is running game, I'ma drag that ass! Watch!"

Chapter 5

It had been some time since Rayven's ad was placed on the internet, and the mail was rolling in. His ad was doing good. He had received several letters from both women and men. Some letters contained photos, but most didn't.

"Like I was saying, prison is the closest you will ever come to death without being dead," Rayven spoke as he washed up behind the bedsheet that hung across the cell. It was a homemade curtain that gave a cell buddy a little more private time. They had just finished doing some pushups together. "Jail is the gravesite, and when the judge bangs the gavel, it's no different than the preacher throwing the first batch of dirt. It's all final. Trial is like the funeral service, people talking about the good and bad in your life."

"Man, you're crazy as shit," Moon said. They had been locked down for four days after the stabbing death of a fellow inmate. They had been covering everything from rehabilitation and slavery, to snitching, menticide, and recidivism, over the course of the lockdown.

Moon waited until after Rayven finished washing up, then got his turn. It was still jive early. They hadn't even passed mail out yet. "Turn the news on," Moon said as he took the curtain down and started to fold it. His hands were still wet.

"You can't watch two TVs at once." Rayven picked up his remote and turned on his fifteen-inch, flat-screen television. Truthfully, Rayven hated turning on his TV before six o'clock.

"I can walk, chew gum, talk, and listen to you."

"Yeah, okay."

"I know one thing; I will be glad when this shit is over." Moon had no problem being on lockdown, but he liked it better when it was his own work. "That shit wasn't that serious. You got lucky. He only hit Slim once. He wasn't even trying to kill that nigga." Moon had seen better work. Very rarely did a stabbing impress him. Shit! He had his own bones in the dirt.

"We're the last building. They already finished shaking down and interviewing all the other buildings."

Rayven had gotten his information from another convict on the tier who had a cell phone and had talked to some of the other convicts in other buildings. The dude sent Rayven a kite (letter) on the line with several pieces of ripped sheet with a book tied on the front end that was heavy enough to help it slide across the floor. "We just have to wait our turn. Don't start crying."

"Crying? What's that? I don't even know what a tear looks like." Moon laughed. "I just want to be done with it. Let these bitches shake down and open this bitch back up. I know we have to get interviewed."

"I ain't even going out. I ain't got no rap. I mean, this is prison. Shit is going to happen. Niggas gonna get hit. They're gonna fight and all that other shit. You are talking about twelve hundred different personalities."

"No doubt. I ain't going out either." Moon wasn't sure if they could refuse to come out. He knew they didn't have to talk. "Fuck that shit."

...these niggas ain't wanted me home, these niggas was looking for love, hollering free me on songs but really they wanted me gone. Came home nobody dailing my phone, now I'm on a mission. I'm up in my zone. These niggas were ducking me, label was fucking me....

"Moon, what's up with you and your old head? I ain't seen you hollering at him lately." Moon had Rayven listening to Boosie Badazz's 'Whispered Desires. Rayven kind of liked it. It was something different, which was cool with him because Moon had been Tupac-ing him to death. If it wasn't *All Eyes On Me*, it was *Makaveli* or *Still I Rise*.

Moon was pacing the floor of the cell. It was something that most guys did when the institution was locked down. It was a form of exercise.

"Fuck that nigga!" Moon barked, looking at Rayven seated on his bunk to be sure he got the picture.

"Damn! I thought that was your man?"

"He was, but that nigga phony. People need to start liking niggas for who they are, not who they want them to be." Moon really wanted to put that knife in the older dude who used to be like an uncle and teacher to him.

"Why do you say that he's phony?" Rayven asked curiously. The good thing about Rayven was that he didn't have a problem learning from people, young or old. He would sit at anybody's feet if they could teach him something.

Moon went on to explain why he had stopped fucking with the old head. He said that whenever he was on some negative shit, the old head got on him about it, telling him why that wasn't the way. So on and so on. Moon also explained how, when he did do something positive, the old head still criticized him, telling him his ideas wouldn't work and how stupid they were.

"It's like he just wants to see me fail." Moon waited for Rayven's response.

Rayven knew a lot of the older guys in prison were set in their ways and often miserable. They hated the fact that they didn't matter anymore, but it was the fact that the kids nowadays those days didn't fall at their feet that killed them. "Moon, it's hard for a lot of these old dudes to see young soldiers as equals."

"That's why they stay getting crushed in here and in the streets." Moon didn't like that. He was a man, too. "He ain't done anything that I ain't done. Not shit. Yeah, he paved the way for some shit, and I respect that, but that's where it stops. That's it."

Rayven knew too many niggas were trying to live off that old shit. The new kids respected the past but didn't submit to it. They followed actions instead of talking. "I feel you. There's nothing new under the sun. All older guys ain't like that though. You do have the ones like myself, the ones who view men, young and old, as equals until they show that they don't deserve that view."

"A lot of niggas get their heads hit, thinking that young niggas can't tell them shit."

"True. That was why the dude got stabbed the other day."

Knock, knock, knock.

Moon and Rayven looked up to see a male correctional officer at the door with a few pieces of mail in his hand. All views were forgotten once the officer started calling their names. Moon received two pieces, and Rayven got four.

"Alexander!" the CO called when Moon turned to walk away.

"Yo?" Moon turned to face the CO.

"Here." He knelt down and slid a new issue of the *B-More Flawless* magazine underneath the door that had one of his big homies on the cover.

"Oh, shit! They got my man, R.I.C.H. Mike from Cherry Hill on the cover!" Moon said, looking at the photograph of Mike and his beautiful wife standing outside of one their R.I.C.H. Bars."

"Here, yo." Moon tossed Rayven his mail and threw his own on his bed before sitting down to flip through the *Flawless* Magazine. It was like he couldn't wait to read on his big homie. Other dudes on the tiers were starting to yell out of cell doors also once the magazines slid underneath the door. "They got your man Captain Andrew from 'We Our Us' in here too." Moon stopped flipping through the magazine to show Rayven to picture.

"Oh, yeah?" Rayven looked up to see the photograph of a large group of men, women, and children, and immediately spotted Captain Andrew. "Yeah, let me check that out when you're done," Rayven requested, recognizing quite a few people in the crowd. He saw his cousin Anthony Muhammad from the Nation of Islam, his old Pastor Ebony from South Baltimore, and a few guys he knew from Baltimore Brothers.

"I got you," Moon assured and went back to flipping through the magazine.

Rayven began flipping through his mail. There was a letter from some chick in Jersey, one from some dude in Texas, and the last two were from his mother and daughter. That made him smile. One piece of mail in prison could make a person feel very loved. "Who hit you?" Rayven asked.

Moon set the *B-More Flawless* Magazine down and picked up the two pieces of mail. "My baby, Pooh. Who else?" It was one letter and a 'thinking of you' card.

Rayven respected how Pooh got at her man. She held that nigga down. It wasn't always easy, but it was love. "One Love and my Rib hit me. Plus, I got two hits off the internet."

"I heard that, playa. Your pen game must be like that." Moon started flipping through the magazine again. He always waited to read wifey's mail before he went to bed. "Oh, shit Look!" Moon stopped on a page with a chick on it that looked very familiar

Rayven looked down as Moon stood up to show him the magazine. "Okay, am I supposed to know who that is?"

"What?" Moon looked at him like he was crazy. "That's T-Savage from the city. Shorty that. She be putting on for the city, too, spitting that fire. And she's pretty as fuck! My nieces turned me on to her. Seeing shorty in this joint is like, damn! First R.I.C.H. Mike, now shorty." Moon handed the open *King* to Rayven. Moon liked seeing people from Baltimore make it because 95 percent of them always kept it real.

"Damn, shorty is bad," Rayven admitted, looking at T-Savage. There weren't too many bitches that could get away with short hair. "Best female rapper of the year, huh?"

"Absolutely."

"Okay." Rayven nodded respectfully. "I like that."

"Ah, nigga, don't try to claim my folks." Moon grabbed the magazine out of Rayven's hands. Dudes in prison always tried claim the baddest bitches out of magazines as their own. Some niggas even hung photos all over their cell walls and acted like the bitch was their real girl.

"Bruh, you already know that I like my women thick like Michelle Obama, thorough like Angela Davis, and bad like Kim Bryant."

"True," Moon admitted as he decided to let Rayven read his mail. He knew that Rayven had a thing for mature women.

While Rayven read his mail, he was tripping. He couldn't understand what was wrong with the homosexuals. His ad actual said women only. However, he still had homo-thugs writing him. Rayven threw the letter in the corner by the door after balling it up. He couldn't even read anymore. How could a grown ass man try to prey on another grown ass man in prison? That was some sick shit.

"Ayo, I am thinking about entering this *Flawless* magazine." Rayven just looked at him like he'd lost about the letter. "What?"

"I said I'm thinking of entering this rap competition in the *Flawless*."

"Do you."

"What cha mean, do you? You think I'm joking?" Moon waited for a response. "You really think shit is a joke, don't you? I could have made it in the rap game, but I went out in the streets."

"Okay, let me hear something then," Rayven called his bluff.

"Okay, check this." Moon spun around and faced the wall mirror. "Okay, let's get it. Un, un."

"Hold up, dog!" Rayven was laughing. "Why are you looking into the mirror?"

"I'm getting into my zone. Just listen."

"Alright."

"50 Cent! 50-50-50-50 Cent, you're a rat homie. Might as well go cry, homeboy. Go look to the sky, homie. Have mercy on you; have mercy on your soul! 'Cause everybody know you told. 50 Cent! 50-50-50-50 Cent, you're a rat, homie." Moon was licking and biting his lips while clutching his jaws and shit, getting into the mood. "50 Cent, you a pussy nigga. You should have been dead, lying, knowing niggas ain't put no funds on your head. Won't you just kill yourself, weak ass nigga. You that snake in the grass; you just ain't been found. You that underground rat. You just ain't been crowned. When you rhyme, somebody gets snitched on every time. You are the greatest, something like Sammy the Bull in his prime." Moon breathed. "You walk the block with your bundles, wired down on the humble, running down to homicide, telling them cops what that gon' do, trying to trick, man. Go right ahead. Keep playing them games. Your family better be scared! But then again, your baby moms cut you off 'cause she knows what you did."

"I can't lie, bruh, that shit was tight." Rayven was impressed.

"Yeah. I can do a little something." Moon was still looking at himself in the mirror. "I am the shit! One of the realest young niggas alive. I ain't never went sour…" Moon mumbled underneath his beath.

"So who hit you off the net?"

"Some little faggie from Texas." Rayven clutched his jaw at the thought. "I would slap the shit out of him if I could."

"Them gumps be thinking that a nigga in the joint will accept anything."

"They got the game fucked up. I told you, life is about integrity. Either you have it, or you don't," Rayven spoke from the heart. "I don't fuck around with no men. I am all man. I ain't never went against that in any form, and that's how I'm going to my grave."

"But you have to admit, some of these busters make us look bad. They be on that undercover shit, creeping around, fucking with boys on the low."

"They don't make us look bad. They aren't cut like me, nor are they anything like me. A man walks securely. If a man is doing something he is ashamed of, he shouldn't be doing it. That's what weak ass niggas do. People do and don't do shit, according to their integrity. People do what they can live with. They have to look in the mirror. That goes for the rat, the prostitute, the gump, etcetera." The veins in Rayven's neck were popping up as he spoke.

"So you're telling me it's not the code that truly stops a person in the game from snitching?"

"Nope."

"So, if it's not the code of honor, then what is it?"

"It's the heart, the morals and principles, which is all a part of integrity, and as far as the game goes with the code, I am not speaking of a person who's not a part of the life. I'm speaking of the ones playing the game. I've been in this game all my life. I don't know how a civilian thinks. I know that a rat is a person who is part of our world, a coward who rats on friends, family, and foe to save his ass. Civilians are snitching when they tell the police that someone grabbed their hard-earned money. A rat gives up information for nothing, information that has nothing to do with anything and is unknown. Still, at the end of the day, no matter who they are, they have to lay with themselves. Some can live with it, some can't. But no matter what, it will always be with them. Every time a man calls a rat out, it will be directed to them."

"I agree, but what about the faggies?" Moon knew Rayven could quickly get off track when speaking of rats.

"In some ways, I can respect a gump who is open about it because that's who he is. It's that down-low shit I hate. How can a man roll like that? The undercover gumps are the worst kind. I truly hate them chumps for their ways—running around like men all day but wanting that log at night. If I can't live with my actions if someone I loved found out, then I ain't being me. Most importantly, you have to be able to live with yourself. Look at the dudes around here, writing these gumps," Rayven said. "Motherfuckers ain't got no integrity. Niggas will do anything for a dollar. You can't ever trust a nigga like that. Even the Bible speaks on that in Proverbs 10:9; it says he who walks with integrity walks securely, but he who perverts his ways will become known."

"Like that nigga Walter Hall down the tier." Moon spoke of a cold-blooded rat who slept down the tier. He'd let a homo-thug with cornrows named Mike Moses suck his dick for a hundred dollars and some commissary.

"Exactly. Niggas be writing sex letters and all that shit just for a few dollars or for reasons that they are unwilling to admit, even to themselves. How do you even come up with that sick shit in your head?"

"A lot of dudes think it will never come out."

"Sixty percent of the time, it won't. But look at that Jamaican nigga Chris who got caught with the toothbrush holder stuck in his ass." Rayven had to laugh at the memory of the go-hard Rasta who got jammed up by a female officer with his legs in the air. "When it does come out, how do they defend it? That's why I haven't done anything that I am ashamed of behind these walls."

"Oh, they're going to say that 'we was just working 'em,'" Moon said, thinking of the most used line in prison when it came to dealing with rats and boys alike.

"But you and I know men don't live like that. Men do them. They don't do anything in the dark that they wouldn't do in the light."

"No matter who a nigga is, that shit takes away from your character. Fuck all that 'I'm not catching, I'm pitching' shit! Fuck how hard a nigga go! Fuck how many people he killed or women he fucked. If he fucking with them boys, he's a faggie—plain and simple."

"Ain't no question," Rayven said.

"Let me ask you this." Moon paused until Rayven was waiting for the question. "What about two women? What's that called?'

"Sexy as shit. That's the shit. Two women. There's nothing wrong with that. Women are beautiful. There's only one thing sexier than one woman."

"And what's that?" Moon was curious as to what could possibly be better than a beautiful woman.

"Two." Rayven smirked.

"Man. That's a double standard," Moon said. "But I'm with you, dog." They both laughed and went on kicking it about another subject.

* * * * *

"Think about it, Moon. Everybody can't have five or six murders under their belts." Rayven was peeping out the crack of the cell door at the COs at the front of the tier, shaking down. Both Rayven and Moon had refused to be interviewed the day before.

It was 8:30 a.m. on a Wednesday morning when they started shaking down on Rayven and Moon's tier. They had about six more cells before it would be their turn. The COs were moving jive fast. Rayven and Moon had been up since about six o'clock, putting up their dirt and contraband.

"Man, I'm telling you, when I was on the hopper tier, more than half of the tier had bodies," Moon assured him.

"Yeah, but how many of them had rap buddies— co-defendants?"

"A few."

"I'm telling you, if everybody on your tier had five bodies, that's like seventy times five. Think about it. The murder rate hadn't reached three hundred in a few years at that time. So somebody was lying."

"So why would them niggas say that?"

"Listen. Some of them might have been truthful, most weren't. So, 85 percent of the time, dudes get locked up on their first murder case and start acting like they got a grave yard full of bodies. The problem is that nobody except maybe the dude with a few bodies under his belt wants to be the guy doing life for one murder. Out of every ten dudes doing time or charged with murder, two, maybe three of them got more than one murder."

"So, there's a lot of lying going on?" Moon started thinking about the guys who were around him who weren't serving time for murder. They always said they had bodies to try and be down. What damn fool wanted to send himself to prison?

"Well, you got to let guys have their realities because you got yours."

"I guess I feel that. It's like the guy who knows he is never going home but continues to tell himself otherwise."

T9hey talked for a few more minutes, then lay back in their own thoughts and waited to be shaken down, both silently praying that the guards didn't find the knives or work. Either way, at the end of the day, they both knew that it was better to get jammed up with it than to find themselves in a jam without it.

"Okay, gentlemen. Time to cuff up," the male officer said, popping (opening) the slot where the bag lunches and trays came in and trash went out when the jail was on lockdown.

Rayven was the first to be cuffed up. He stood at the back of the cell as Moon turned his back to the cell door and allowed the officer to handcuff him through the slot.

"Open cell one fourteen," the male officer said into his walkie-talkie after looking into the cell again through the glass window to be sure that Rayven and Moon were secured in their handcuffs. "Back out of the cell slowly."

"Lewis and Alexander, right?" another officer asked so she could check their cell off of the shake-down list.

"Yeah."

"Okay. One at a time. Walker, y'all strip Lewis first," another light-skinned male officer said, grabbing Moon's handcuff chain between the cuffs as a form of control.

Moon stood outside his cell while four correctional officers entered the cell, two removing their mace to strip Rayven like some scared bitches.

They removed Rayven's cuffs and proceeded to search his clothes as he took them off. Nothing made a man feel more fucked up than having to strip for male officers. Some of them chumps were real dick watchers, and they'd be trying to get their shit off.

"Man, I already squatted once. I ain't doing it again." Rayven stood his ground. One thing about him was that he would go in on the police just like he would go in on an inmate, prisoner, or convict.

"Oh, you gonna—"

"Hold up, McMullen," Officer Walker cut his fellow officer off. He knew Lewis didn't fuck with anyone, but he was a threat. Not only that. He also knew that if they jumped on him, other convicts would go off. "It's cool, Lewis. Get dressed."

Rayven started putting his shit back on.

"Dick watcher." Moon couldn't help himself. He tried to hold his tongue, but McMullen was a certified bitch and dick watcher. Moon knew, as did Walker, that Rayven would crush him easily. McMullen was the type that saw your dick and got mad because it was bigger than his. “What? You mad because you seeing the dick your wife goes crazy over?”

McMullen’s wife, also a correctional officer, was crazy for a big dick, and everybody knew it. The bitch was known for running up on the showers and opening cell doors while guys were using the bathroom, chasing dick.

“Watch your mouth, Alexander, before you get a disrespect infraction,” McMullen spoke as his face twisted up. His co-workers laughed and snickered.

Moon smirked and got stripped before being placed next to Rayven in a chair facing the open cell door so they could watch the officers searching their cell. “It’s not my fault that you have to tell your kids that Daddy dick watches for a living.”

“Man, put my shit back!” Moon barked as one of the officers left his clothes on the bed. Mullen was going extra hard.

“Be cool, Moon.” Rayven looked at him.

Moon picked up on what Rayven was doing, but his plan was to keep them on edge so that they didn’t find the hammers (knives) they had stashed in the cell. Rayven was silent as one of the officers came in contact with his hammer, and all that he was thinking was that he had to beat them.

Rayven watched as he got lucky again. There was really no such thing as a good stash spot in prison. What was good one day might not be good the next. It really came down to how lazy the officer was most of the time.

A nigga definitely wasn’t trying to lose his visits for a simple knife ticket. If a nigga had to go down, let it be for putting in some work. That was Moon’s motto.

“Captain! We got something!”

Rayven’s heart stopped until he realized it was the cell next door to them where the female officer spoke of finding something. Rayven could see another CO holding something that looked like a sword instead of a knife, and the female had a cell phone in her hand.

"Damn! Where the fuck Poochie and Country get that steel from?" someone yelled out.

The cell phone was nothing. Rayven made eye contact with his next-door neighbors. He knew if one of them didn't take the beef, they were both going down. No matter what, one or both of them would be doing lock-up time for at least 150 days.

All Rayven thought about was how many times they had beaten the shakedown, but he knew they couldn't beat them bitches all the time.

"Okay, fellers," Walker said as they stepped from the cell. It was at that moment that Rayven peeped that most of the SRT (Special Response Team) had shaken him down—Brown, Walker, and Taylor. Taylor was fucking one of the phattest and baddest officers in the jail, so he never went out of his way to fuck with a nigga, nor did the white boy, Brown. They just did their eight as sure as Rayven did his twenty-four. *Damn!*

"Good," Moon said. "Get this buster away from my cell." Moon mugged McMullen. Moon wished that it had been McMullen who caught that knife last month.

Their cell was tossed. Shit was everywhere, but neither Rayven nor Moon was mad. Shid, they both came off with their hammers, and that alone was something to be happy about.

"Let's get this mess cleaned up," Rayven said, looking around.

"No doubt." Moon started picking things up. "Did you see niggas sliding their hammers out?"

"Yeah. Niggas are fools. I would rather get jammed with it than get in a jam without it any day."

"You and me both."

"Hit the music while we get this shit right," Rayven instructed. "And turn it up."

* * * * *

"What the fuck? Am I supposed to feel contrite or something because some kid got stabbed to death? This is a penitentiary," Rayven was saying over a chess game with John-Boy. John-Boy knew that Rayven was flagrant when it came to speaking his mind.

The jail had been off lockdown for a few days, so it was business as usual. John-Boy was getting on Rayven because the kid who was stabbed to death's uncle, who was also in the jail, owed Rayven fifteen dollars for some weed, and he was applying pressure about his money.

"I'm just saying, have a heart. His nephew just got stabbed to death." John-Boy wanted Rayven to be cool. He knew Rayven was stubborn when it came to his beliefs about something. John-Boy remembered how Rayven tied a New York nigga up at another jail when he needed some money. He could only imagine what he would do when a nigga actually owed him some.

Rayven looked at John-Boy. He was one of the few men Rayven truly respected and would hear out. "I'll give him some time."

No more needed to be said. When a man gave his word, it was honored. Men respected men.

"I need to go call my uncle Junior." Rayven got up in the middle of their chess game. "I will be back."

"Give Sidney my regards."

Rayven walked up the dayroom steps to the phone as he dug in his pocket to remove his phonebook.

"Hey, Auntie Brook," Rayven said after he heard his uncle Sidney's wife accept the collect call.

"Hey, baby," his aunt replied. "How's everything going?"

"Fine. Uncle Junior home?"

"He sure is. Hold on," she said a few seconds before he heard her calling his uncle.

"Nephew, what's good?" Uncle Junior's raspy voice cracked over the phone.

"Not too much, Uncle Junior. You know the deal."

Sidney Junior had fought for his freedom back in the late eighties and won. Then he went home, graduated from Morgan State, became a coach, and married a fine ass Baltimore City public school principle. "How's the family?"

"Everybody is good. Delia is still crazy too. Kenneya and India still getting on my nerves, and Na'Kya one of them, I don't know what you call it when you do some type of Muslim girl training with the Nation of Islam."

"Oh, M.G.T.," Rayven corrected.

"Yeah, that M-G-stuff, " Sidney agreed. "Besides that, everybody waiting for you to come home."

"I'll be there soon," Rayven assured when truthfully, the truth was a lot more complicated. To be honest, Rayven didn't know when or even if he was ever coming home. However, he knew that his uncle understood exactly what he was saying—that he would continue to fight for his freedom until he was dead or free.

They chit-chatted for a minute about life, the work Uncle Junior was doing in the community and school system, and the future. "Look, I got to get up to this school. We're playing Connexions today, and my kids would kill me if I missed our championship game, but I'ma hit your lawyer with some bread in the next few weeks."

"A'ight, thanks, Unc. That's a good look. My post will be filed soon too. I know I got these people this time," Rayven declared. "Oh yeah, your man sends his regards also."

"Who? John-Boy?" Sidney questioned, thinking about his old penitentiary partner and jailhouse lawyer.

"You know it," Rayven confirmed.

"He still stuck in the seventies?" Uncle Junior laughed.

"Absolutely." Rayven shook his head, thinking about all the conversations he and John-Boy had about the eighties—the women, the times, and the change.

"Yell at my man for me," Uncle Junior encouraged.

"Will do."

"Hey, look, I have to go. I love you, champ. I'ma give the phone back to your aunt Brook," Uncle Junior explained. "Just let her know everything and I got you."

"Definitely." Rayven knew his uncle was a cold G when it came to any form of the game. Growing up, people used to always compare him to his uncle. Rayven had the pleasure of jailing with him for a few years and witnessing his work.

"You can't save the game."

"Yeah. You're right. Fat Bryant told me the same thing the other day." Outlaw knew that his nephew was right.

"How is Slim doing?"

"He good, trying to survive his last two years."

"Oh, yeah. Bird yelled at you." Rayven changed the subject because he really wanted his uncle to stay in the streets. He wouldn't be good for anything back on his side of the fence.

"Holler at him for me." Outlaw spoke of the man's man and warrior.

"Love you more, Unc. Walk slow, think fast," Rayven said. "The phone about to hang up anyway."

"A'ight, bet. You take care and stay focused," was the last thing that Rayven heard before the phone line went died.

Rayven stood there for a moment before hanging up. He had forgotten to tell his uncle about new Supreme Court ruling.

Rayven walked back downstairs to the chess game. John-Boy was still sitting there, studying the board.

"Let's see if thirty minutes of studying can help you." Rayven sat down.

"It was my game when you got up." John-Boy made his move. "Checkmate, big mouth!"

"John-Boy, let me ask you something," Rayven said as they were waiting to lock in for the night.

"What's up? I hope you're not still stuck on how I pulled off that checkmate."

"Nah, this don't have anything to do with chess. It's just something Moon and I were discussing, and I wanted to hear your thoughts on it."

"Shoot."

"What's your thoughts on rats and faggies?'

"Being a homosexual in the streets is cool if you're open with it, but only weak, moralless niggas fuck with boys in the joint as an excuse to try to hide who they truly are. A true man knows that you should never do anything you can't do out in the open or tell your family about. A handful of the so-called men in prison do shit behind these walls that they would never do if the outside world could see them. They still go hard and all, but the truth of the matter is that they are weak men with no morals. They are not what true men call 'A Man's Man'. You see, Rayven, the true measure of a man is what he does when he feels or knows he won't be found out."

"Yeah. In a nutshell, that's how I put it," Rayven revealed.

"And the rats. Where do I start? They are much more open now. It's the new 'in'. They have become a part of the game because they stopped being dealt with. It's a shame. Rats have always been around and always will be. However, when they ratted back in my day, they got handled or cut off. There was no in-between. You were either a man or a bitch when shit hits the fan, plain and simple."

"Nowadays, dudes rat and get TV shows and shit made after them. They come home, still hang around the same neighborhoods that they told in without consequence, and they're still loved."

"But so many things are different today. Dudes leave their friends behind bars, fuck their man's girl, and never get punished when the guy shows again. They roll up on them in the streets like ain't nothing ever happened. There is no code today. There's only what you say and what you do. Today, you are allowed to return to the game, even after you snitch. As long as you ain't tell on more than one very well-known dude, you cool."

"And what about us? What about the last of the dying breed? The legends, the O'G.'s, and men still cut from that old cloth?" Rayven asked.

"We have to cherish each other, educate others, and crush anybody who violates what we stand for. Especially the so-called men who go against the old laws for these new jack rules because they know better. It's like every time that I turn around, a so-called man finds a reason to play for the other team, so don't be surprised who's the next one to pop up on the wrong side of the courtroom. We are losing numbers every day."

Rayven just shook his head and remained silent. He had to let that marinate.

Chapter 6

A year would pass in no time. It was Buttons' nineteenth birthday. Buttons and Keisha were in their last year of school. Yusra was talking about getting married, and Nichelle was still off the hook.

"Damn, girl. I can't believe we are all grown. After this last year of school, it's party time," Keisha said, waving her drink all over the place, spilling it on the floor. She was drunk as shit off the Don Julio Reposado shots.

They were at Keisha's house, having a good time. People were everywhere, and there were all kinds of drinks and edibles being passed around.

The music was jumping from one of those new Bluetooth speakers, and people were dancing and grinding on each other.

"I know. I can't wait." Buttons started shaking her ass and moving her hips in a circular motion. She was nursing a glass of Grand Marnier. "Where the fuck is my man at?" Buttons looked around for Josh as the lights flashed on and off. The last time she'd laid eyes on him, he'd been in the middle of the dance floor with a bottle Ace in his hand and some little thot all in his face.

"I'm about to cum," Josh confessed, looking down to watch the little nasty bitch's lips as they hugged his dick. "Shit!" Josh threw his head back. Shorty's head was fire. He couldn't remember her name, but he knew that she was one of Buttons' homegirls.

"Cum in my mouth," she begged before stuffing the dick back down her throat as far as it would go. They were inside of a dark bedroom on the second floor of Keisha's house, up to no good, lips and hands in places they didn't belong.

"Hmmm." The nameless thot moaned as Josh's brother long-dicked her from the back.

"You got some good pussy." Josh's brother began pushing his dick slowly in and out of her hot, wet pussy as if trying to savor every stroke.

She stopped sucking Josh's dick long enough to look back over her shoulder like Halle Berry in the movie *Monster's Ball* when she was about to get hit from the back and bit her bottom lip as if to say, 'I know my shit is good.'

Buttons grabbed another shot of Don and started walking around, looking for Josh.

"Buttons!" Yusra called just as Buttons was about to go upstairs.

"Huh?"

"What the fuck are you doing?"

"Trying to find my man." Buttons looked around again.

"Girl, forget that nigga. Everybody knows that Josh is community dick. Besides, it's your birthday, not his." Yusra grabbed Buttons' hand and pulled her back toward the dance floor.

Buttons started dancing with two dudes, and they were all over her. She was holding her drink in the air as she put it on the two guys who sexually grinded into her.

"Come on!"

"Work them niggas, girl! They ain't ready!" Yusra screamed as she watched her girl handle the two guys on the dance floor.

"I got 'em." Buttons was in the groove, feeling good.

Yusra locked eyes with Nichelle as she sneakily came down the steps and made her way over to her. "Girl, what the fuck are you up to?"

"Nothing. I just came from the bathroom." Nichelle rolled her eyes.

"The bathroom?"

"Yes, bitch, the bathroom!" Nichelle snapped. "Don't start, Yusra."

"I ain't start shit. What are you jumpy for?" Yusra looked up and saw Josh and his brother coming from upstairs. "Oh, lookie, lookie." Yusra lifted up one of her eyebrows.

Nichelle followed her eyes and saw the two brothers making their way across the room. It was Knocky and Josh. "So what do they have to do with me?"

"You tell me. You know what? Whatever, Nichelle. Some kind of friend you are. You are a nasty bitch, and I don't know why Buttons and Keisha even fuck with you. You are poison." Yusra was ready to drag Nichelle's ass up in there because she knew that she had been up to no good. She just couldn't prove it.

"Stop thinking I'm evil. I hope you don't go starting no crazy shit, saying untrue things out your mouth. Regardless of what you think of me, I love Buttons and Keisha and would never cross them for no dick." She looked at Josh so Yusra could get the point.

"Look, Ms. Thang." Yusra faced Nichelle and stepped into her personal space, daring her to act up. "I'm a lot of things, but a snitch ain't one of them. Please believe that. If I caught you stabbing my girl in the back, the truth is gonna be written all over your face and body from the ass whipping I give you." With that said, Yusra turned and walked away, leaving Nichelle to her own thoughts.

"Whatever, bitch!" Nichelle had to get the last word. She wasn't sweating Yusra's little ass. Besides, Yusra knew that she wasn't no slouch. Nichelle just knew how shit got started.

The party was winding down and starting to clear out. There were only a few stragglers inside, but most people were either out front or gone. Beer cans, liquor bottles, weed wrappings, and used vapes littered the sidewalk out front. There had even been two used condoms found upstairs.

"You ready, baby?" Buttons asked Josh as he held her in a couple's bear hug from behind.

"Yeah." Josh was ready to run up in her. To him, she was nothing but pussy, good pussy, but pussy nevertheless. When he said girlfriend, he really meant that. Buttons was just a friend who happened to be a girl. "We're gonna catch a ride with my brother."

"I don't care. I'm just ready to go." Buttons had that drunk horniness.

Buttons and Josh climbed into his brother's car and headed to her house since she knew that nobody was home.

* * * * *

"Look. Hold the cell down for me," Rayven said. Shit was about to go down. Rayven was about to go to war with another well-known knife-slinger. The dude had been playing games with Rayven, giving him the runaround on a nice piece of money. Shit came to a head the day before, when Rayven dusted him off with his hands in the gym bathroom after he told Rayven that he would have to get it in blood.

Although Rayven had fucked him up with the hands, he still wanted the nigga off the compound because he didn't trust him now. He knew that the nigga would try some fuck shit, so one of them had to go.

Marlboro was a dude out of Maryland, claiming DC, but Rayven knew the truth. His cousin, Buckey Fields, was in the feds, and it was known that Maryland niggas always acted like they were from DC. For years, niggas called it a Baltimore/DC war when shit jumped off in the Annex or Cut, when truthfully, it was Baltimore against Maryland. Ninety percent of the Maryland niggas just wanted to be from DC because Baltimore was one of the only places recognized out of Maryland in the gangster world as a threat. Only true men from Maryland claimed their true hood because they overstood that it wasn't where you were from but how you stood tall that mattered.

Knowing that men came from all over, Rayven knew that it was only a few real DC niggas in the Annex, and he fucked with almost all of them. They'd just gotten jammed up in Maryland somewhere.

"You already know that I got you. Give me whatever you want me to bring to you while you're down in A-building." Moon worked on lockup, so Rayven would be easy to get to.

By now, Moon was rockin' a bald head just like Rayven. The only difference between the two was that Moon wore a sky-blue soldier rag every day.

"Everything I want is in that bag." Rayven pointed to a net bag under the bunk.

"I got you." Moon really wanted to put the work in for Rayven because the week before, Rayven had stepped in to assist him when he got caught slipping by a known knockout artist. The nigga was nice with his hands, but Moon was nice with the knife.

"Give me some love." Rayven looked at Moon like a brother. They had been in the cell together for well over a year now. They had their disagreements, but it was all love.

"Shid, nigga, I'm going with you." Moon couldn't see himself watching his brother go to war alone. The last time Moon went on lockup, it was for his man Oatmeal. Oatmeal had stabbed another well-known BGF member, and it was on. It was Moon, Oatmeal, and his big homie, Bugg-eye from Cherry Hill, against half of the compound.

"Nah, soldier." Rayven felt Moon's pain. Marlboro was a tested vet, and any time two men went to war, only a few things could result, the worst being a death sentence, the weakest being somebody tapping out in the heat of battle.

Rayven knew, in prison, you were only considered as serious as your last victim or the last nigga you went up against.

"You're right. It's your beef." Moon knew that the worst kind of nigga was the one who let his man get crushed on his watch. Niggas were going to hate no matter what. Moon would rather be criticized for jumping into a knife fight than for letting his man get murked in one. "But remember, you said that steel sharpens steel."

"Let me pray." Rayven closed his eyes, knowing what could happen once he hit the yard. Rayven didn't have a religious preference, having studied them all yet falling in line with none. He only believed that there was something greater than himself. Choosing his words from the great Greek philosopher Fredrick Nietzsche, Rayven prayed in his head.

If death is a removal from here to some other place, and if what we are told is true—that all of the dead are there—what greater blessing could there be than this? To die in the heart of battle. It would be a specially interesting experience to join them there. To meet George and Johnathan Jackson, The Most Honorable Elijah Muhammad, Noble Drew Ali, and all the other heroes or warriors of their day, who met their death through unfair trials or as martyrs. To compare my fortunes with theirs would be rather amusing, I think; and above all, I should like to spend my time there as I do here, in examining and searching people's minds to find out who is really wise among them, and who only thinks that they are.

"Amen." Rayven opened his eyes, ready for war.

"Okay, y'all got five minutes to get wherever you're going," Ms. Hopkins said as the doors opened for morning recreation right after Rayven prayed.

So far, it seemed like the gods were on his side. Rayven stepped out and looked Ms. Hopkins right in her eyes. "Be good." he mumbled.

Ms. Hopkins instantly knew something was wrong. Rayven waited for her to get on the shakedown line and went to her. Dhaka felt what she thought was a jailhouse shake. She couldn't be sure, because Rayven had big legs. Something was up.

She patted him down again before he walked off toward the yard. She wanted to turn him in, say that he had a weapon, but she knew that, no matter what, he would get in trouble, so she just hoped he would be okay. She knew that he was a man, through and through, and trusted that he could take care of himself.

Rayven's heart was pumping extra blood as he entered the yard. The outcome of war was always unknown. There was just a commitment to death and hope of coming out with life.

Moon was right beside him.

"Showtime!" Rayven whispered to Moon, spotting Marlboro near the weights. Rayven kneeled as if he was lacing his boots and retrieved his knife. He slipped it into his sleeve after making sure the rope tied to it was securely wrapped around his wrist.

Rayven then stood up and made his way toward the weights. He was prepared to die for his respect. They had taken everything else from him—his family, his freedom, and his identity. He would never let anyone take his respect.

"Let me holler at you, Rayven," Marlboro said as he approached. Marlboro acted like he had forgotten about all the bitches and whores that he had called Rayven before going on to tell him to suck his dick last night out the cell door on the tier. All of this came after telling Rayven he wasn't getting paid after the fight.

Mistake one.

Rayven kept stepping.

"That shit ain't for us, Slim."

Mistake two.

Nobody is off limits in war.

"So what do you wanna do?" Marlboro realized shit was going down with or without him fighting back.

Mistake three.

Marlboro waited too long to commit himself. Rayven drew his steel, and it was work call.

Marlboro never had a chance. He even dropped his knife in the heat of battle.

"You bitch!" he screamed when Rayven stabbed him in the face, just below the eye.

"You still talking shit, nigga?" Rayven was laying that steel up in him.

Moon was standing back, watching with a smirk on his face as Rayven slaughtered Marlboro.

Marlboro went from name-calling to calling for help before he passed out as the COs arrived to help him.

"Oh my God, baby. What have you done?" Dhaka looked at Rayven—who was covered in blood—to the body laying on the ground. She just knew that the guy was dead; he had to be. There was so much blood loss. She couldn't tell if Rayven was hit also, because he just stood there in a daze.

Moon watched, along with the other convicts, inmates, and prisoners in the yard, as they handcuffed Rayven and rushed Marlboro to medical. Marlboro was going to need Medivac if he was still breathing. Moon could tell by looking at him that he was going to be flown to Maryland Shock Trauma. He knew Rayven would be cool if Marlboro didn't die. He hadn't had a ticket in a minute, so he wasn't looking at too much lock-up time—ninety days at the most, hopefully.

* * * * *

"Hurry up, girl!" Keisha yelled from downstairs.

"I'm coming!" Buttons was still fucking with her hair.

It was Monday morning, and they were already late for school. Buttons had overslept for the first time in months.

"Keisha, can you please heat me up a blueberry muffin or something?" Buttons walked past the top of the steps in a black thong with no bra. "My stomach on E."

"You white as shit." Keisha laughed as Buttons crossed at the top of the stairs before she went to the kitchen to fix Buttons something to put on her stomach.

Buttons was in the mirror as she put on some skin-tight, two-tone blue jeans. *Only a few more months of this shit.* Buttons rummaged through her dresser drawer, looking for a nice shirt to match her black Jordan tennis shoes she planned to wear. "Here we go." Buttons selected a black-and-blue Polo shirt.

It took Buttons a full thirty minutes to get dressed.

"Got damn, bitch! You act like it's prom night," Keisha said when Buttons finally came down the steps, ready to go. "The Uber will be pulling up in five minutes."

Buttons went into the kitchen and ate the egg and cheese sandwich Keisha had made for her. "You could have at least toasted the bread." Buttons' mouth was full of eggs. Buttons couldn't imagine life without her girl.

"I got you the next time you're hungry."

Buttons and Keisha headed outside when the Uber pulled up to take them to school. They were too late to fuck with the bus.

It took them another fifteen minutes to get to Southwestern High School from the Avenue. When they pulled up in the parking lot, it was 9:24 a.m., and they had both missed first period. They might both be facing after-school detention from their homeroom teachers.

"Look. Don't wait for me at lunch," Buttons said.

"Okay."

"Plus, I think I might have to stay late. My homeroom teacher be tripping at times."

"Cool. I will just meet you down the way."

"You don't think your teacher going to trip?"

"I don't give a fuck. I ain't staying after school, period."

Throughout the school day, Buttons stayed busy. She tried to duck detention by going back to first period during lunch break, but that didn't work. She also had to make up time for the second period.

Buttons wanted all her credits. She couldn't stand another year of school. It was hard, being one of the only white girls in the school, and the fact that she was pretty only added to the hate.

It was almost four o'clock when Buttons strolled out of the school building. She knew Keisha was long gone because she had stopped by her last period and found out that she did, in fact, have detention. Buttons knew she would have to walk down to Westside Shopping Center to get a ride because she'd left her purse in the house and wasn't about to walk back to get it. Usually, she and Keisha would get an Uber, but she was already gone.

As Buttons walked down Fredrick Road, past the creek and elementary school, cars full of guys were driving by, blowing their horns and saying shit. She was also kind of spooked, as always, because being a white girl walking in a black neighborhood was like being a black in a KKK movie theater. Just when Buttons started to feel like God was on her side, she spotted a reason to be spooked, and the reason spotted her.

Buttons wasn't a chump, far from it. Shit, she grew up all up and down Edmondson Avenue, where she had runs-ins with some of the most thoroughbred bitches in West Baltimore, bitches like Sharmaine, Bean, and Sheena. Buttons kept her cool and kept walking toward the mall. Like any smart warrior, she held her ground, but she didn't ask for trouble. That would've been crazy. She was in their hood. However, she would choose fight over flight; win, lose, or draw.

Buttons watched out the side of her eye as Trina and the rest of the Four Horsemen crossed over to her side of the street. *Bitches ain't going to do shit!* To be safe, Buttons slid her pocket knife around in her pocket so it would be easy to get to if shit jumped.

"This bitch wanna be black bad as shit." The little one was the first to talk. They weren't even three feet behind Buttons.

"Mmmhmm, black friends, black swagger, black dick," Trina added and threw a piece of candy at Buttons that barely missed. Buttons looked back.

"That bitch face red as shit."

Trina was the boldest and was rumored to be the toughest, but Buttons knew all the Four Horsemen could rumble. Trina was popping gum and talking shit. Her glossed lips could make any real nigga's dick hard. The rest of the crew was slowly sucking lollipops.

"Run your mouth now, white girl!" the brown-skinned one barked.

Buttons held her tongue. *Almost there.* To Buttons, the brown-skinned girl was the cutest. Buttons was sure she could take her one-on-one.

"You don't remember me, do you?" The brown-skinned one grabbed Buttons.

"Don't put your hands on me." Buttons faced her with a quickness as Trina and the other two surrounded her.

Strike first, and don't worry about what's behind you. Keisha's words rang in her head.

"Oooh. She's ready to fight. Bitch, please."

"You might remember my taste better than my face." She dug her hand inside of her sweatpants. "Mmmh."

Buttons watched as her eyes rolled into her head somewhere. *I know this bitch ain't finger popping herself.* "What, bitch!" Buttons didn't catch her comment.

"I said, you might know my flavor," she spoke, pulling her hand out of her sweatpants.

Buttons eyed her fingers. She could see traces of what must've been pussy juice. *I wish you would.* Buttons looked her in the eyes. She could feel the blood quickly flowing to her hands. *Bitch, I wish you would.* Buttons dared her with her eyes. Subconsciously, Buttons licked her lips.

"I think this white dyke wants to taste some black pussy. Since you want to be black." Trina sexily ran her fingers through Buttons' hair and lifted it so it could blow in the light wind.

"She already tasted this before."

What the fuck are you waiting for? Buttons asked herself, balling her fists up.

"Yeah, bitch! I was all over Josh's dick that day you said it tasted funny." With that, the brown-skinned chick put her jive wet fingers into Buttons' open mouth. "Remember that? Good, ain't it?"

"That's what men really want."

It took Buttons a split second to realize what had just happened. *Oh, no, she didn't.* It registered fully a moment later.

"Bitch!" Buttons hit her so hard that everybody froze for a second.

"You just fucked up!" Trina barked, and everybody started swinging.

Trina hit Buttons with a mean hook, and her girls followed up. Buttons rumbled with them.

"Hold that bitch!"

"Get the fuck off of my hair!"

"Yeah, what now, bitch!"

"She's biting me!"

"White trash hooker!"

"This for my ancestors, bitch!"

"Yeah, bitch!"

"And I fucked your man!"

They were yelling and talking shit as they threw punch after punch at Buttons' head and body.

"Stomp that bitch!"

Buttons knew she couldn't stay on the ground, no matter what. She finally got to her pocketknife and started swinging it as she made her way back to her feet. She didn't know who she hit, but she knew that she had connected at least once.

"She's got a knife!"

"Oh, shit! That crazy bitch stabbed me!" Trina moaned, grabbing her arm. It was only a flesh wound.

Buttons kept slinging. It was at that moment that the little one realized that her hand was cut too. "I'm cut too!" She eyed Buttons. "Oh, bitch, it's on now."

The brown-skinned one picked up a stick, and the slim, dark-skinned one broke a bottle in half.

"Get that bitch!"

They moved in for the kill.

"Come on." Buttons held her ground with the knife in her hand. She was breathing hard as shit. She was in pain, and she knew that 80 percent of her back would be black, red, and purple in the morning. "Come on. Y'all gonna have to kill me."

"Stop it!" An old dude jumped in between them after the brown-skinned one hit Buttons a few times with the stick.

"Ouch…" Buttons felt the stick again and rushed the girl.

"Please, young lady." The older guy grabbed Buttons almost at the same time that the police and ambulance arrived.

Buttons was hurt the worst. After they were all treated, they were taken into police custody for assault. The old man said that Buttons had the knife and was defending herself. However, she was still charged with two counts of felony attempted murder.

Once they hit the Booking (Central Booking) and were processed, they all got their own recon (release without bail after seeing the commissioner). The Four Horsemen were a lot of things, but snitches weren't one of them. Buttons also kept her mouth shut, saying only that some females jumped her, and it wasn't any of the ones arrested.

Buttons had never been locked up, so her record was clean. Had she had any criminal record, she would have definitely been looking at a bail. The commissioner couldn't deny that she was, in fact, defending herself once he laid eyes on her. All the women in the bullpen kept asking her if she was okay.

Some were even bold enough to say shit like, "Damn! Somebody fucked that white girl up."

They didn't believe she was in for four accounts of attempted murder. "Who you stab? Your husband?" one chick asked, laughing. She didn't know any go-hard white girls from the hood. "Imagine a white girl rumbling some sisters. Bitch, please."

"Whatever." Buttons couldn't stand another fight, but she had to say something. Buttons was sitting in the corner, waiting for her turn on the phone. *Those bitches better know it's on.*

"Hello. Yeah, it's me. I'm charged with attempted murder. Please come and get me. I will tell you when I see you. I only got five minutes. Don't tell my mother. No. Girl, you are a blessing. I love you too." Buttons' spirits were up after her call.

"One minute, Ms. Howard," an officer said.

"Look, I should be out in about an hour. I will. Come on now. I am from the Avenue," Buttons said. "I gotta go. Okay. One hour."

Buttons felt like crying when she got back to the bullpen. *I'm not built for this jail shit.* Buttons couldn't believe that she had been cuffed, photo-ed for a mug shot, and placed in a piss-smelling bullpen with other hard criminals. Women were nodding, scratching, and going through withdrawals. The bullpen/holding cell was small. There was a little three-man concrete bench. However, there were seven women in the little room. The toilet was backed up with what looked like a bloody maxi pad and shit. *I gotta get the fuck out of here.*

Buttons had heard that there were some greasy ass females in the world, but she felt like she had to be trapped in with some of the most trifling women there were.

"Feed up." An ugly, fat, male officer threw some brown paper bags inside the bullpen.

"Fuck no!" Buttons looked inside her bag and saw a frozen cheese and some kind of mystery meat sandwich. She chose only to drink the off-brand apple juice.

They're treating us like dogs.

"You gonna eat your bag, girlfriend?" the same female who had been talking shit asked as soon as she set the bag down. Buttons realized that she was a fiend, and she jive felt sorry for her.

"Nah. Here." Buttons tossed her the bag. She started thinking about all the men reported to be in prison. She said a silent prayer for them. She knew, if it was anything like what she had to endure, they had it bad. There had to be some strong men in prison.

Buttons walked over to the glass and saw three male officers standing in front of another bullpen/holding cell that contained one female. Buttons couldn't fully see her, but it appeared that she was playing with herself for two of the officers while one watched out for the other guards. *Oh my od.* Jail was another world that Buttons knew nothing about. Buttons watched as one of the guards threw an extra bag lunch into the holding cell.

"Howard, let's go," a guard said with too much attitude. Buttons jumped up, as did another chick.

"Brittany Howard," the guard said once she saw two women approaching. "Sit your ass down." She knew Brittany had to be the white girl.

"Can't knock a bitch for trying." She mugged Buttons as if she were mad that she was going instead of her.

It took about forty minutes before Buttons was released. She was so glad she was free that she didn't realize she didn't have a ride. She had been in Booking all day. All of her personal shit was in a clear little Ziploc bag, which she had tucked under her arm. Buttons looked through the Ziploc to see what time it was.

"Damn, it's ten o'clock. I've been here all day," Buttons said, talking to herself as she noticed that her three-hundred-dollar Gucci earrings were missing. *Sneaky ass bitch.* Buttons remembered a female guard who kept peeping her earrings.

Buttons looked up at the sound of a car horn and saw her girl. She walked over to the car and got in.

"What the fuck? " She looked at Buttons' face and knew somebody else had to be fucked up too. "What happened to them?"

"It's a long story," Buttons said and leaned over to give her a tight hug. "I love you." A tear escaped her eye. She felt like she had been gone forever.

"Well, tell it the short way." They pulled off.

Buttons flipped the sun visor down and looked into the little mirror on the back. *Oh, it's on.* Buttons was speechless as she viewed the damage to her face and neck.

"Well, start talking, girl." Yusra was getting impatient, looking at her girl's face. "I just hope this shit not over some nigga!"

As they drove, Buttons gave Yusra the rundown on how shit unfolded. Yusra called Keisha on her cell phone, who called Nichelle after Buttons finished talking. The last thing Buttons heard Yusra say through the open passenger seat window after she dropped her off in front of her house was, "Put a lot of grease in your hair because, come tomorrow, there's going to be a girl fight, and we are the stars." Yusra pulled off, and Buttons entered her mother's house and went right to bed, clothes on and all.

Chapter 7

"Hello. Yeah. Huh? Oh, yeah. Then it's on." Keisha hung up the phone and ran upstairs to wake up her cousin, Six Nine.

'Six Nine' was a big bitch from Park Heights, who could fold a bitch in a B-More minute. Six-Nine had gone to Keisha's house when her cousin informed her that they were looking for some bitches called the Four Horsemen that had jumped her best friend, Buttons.

"Six Nine. Get up, girl," Keisha said, shaking her cousin out of her sleep.

"What, girl? What?" Six Nine looked up. She had been having a good dream.

"Buttons and them are on their way to scoop us. The Four Horsemen bitches are over by Mount Street, so it's on!"

"It's about time! I thought them bitches left town or something." Six Nine was getting homesick.

It had been four days since the after-school incident, and Buttons had been clearing up pretty well for a white girl, but you could still see traces of the ass whipping she had received at the hands of the Four Horsemen. Buttons and them had been looking for Trina and them for a few days. They hadn't shown up to school, so when they got word that Trina and them were on Mount Street, they knew they had to move.

When Buttons, Nichelle, and Yusra arrived, they all entered Keisha's house to put a plan together. The plan was for the Lucky Charms to put in the work while Six Nine recorded it for social media and made sure that nobody jumped in. Plus, Six-Nine was going to hold the car down in case they had to get out of there.

"Look. I want the brown-skinned bitch that hit me with the stick." Buttons was greasing her hair down with some Petroleum Jelly.

"I want all them bitches," Yusra said, standing beside Buttons as she tied her hair down with a scarf. What the fuck is this crazy white girl doing?" Yusra watched as Buttons greased her hair like a black girl, getting ready to rumble and talk shit.

"Buttons, are you sure they are out there?" Keisha didn't feel up to chasing a ghost. The only one they had seen was Trina. They wanted to get her, but Buttons wanted them all at one time.

"Yeah. You know Josh be up there. He said they were sitting out there on Mount Street."

"Call him and make sure they're still out there." Keisha knew that if Josh said they were out there, then they had to be. She also knew that Josh, like all niggas, just wanted to see a girl fight. Shit, it was the only place in Baltimore where you could see ass and titties and sometimes pussy for free. Josh knew, with the Lucky Charms and Four Horsemen rumbling, he was guaranteed to see a lot of extra skin.

"Let's do it." Buttons read the text message. "He said they're still out there.

"Damn, that nigga really wants to see a fight." Yusra looked at Buttons.

"Let's go show him something then," Nichelle, who had been quiet, finally said.

They piled into the car with Six Nine driving. They had on what was known across the city as fighting clothes—dogged Under Armour sneakers, leggings and halter-tops. They had their hair in ponytails and scarves with enough grease to tenderize a turtle's shell.

“Hit the music, bitch,” Yusra said to Nichelle from the back seat where she sat between Buttons and Keisha. Yusra only got on her gangsta shit when somebody fucked with her or her girls.

Nichelle hit the play button, and Glorilla’s latest track started’ rocking the car system.

“Okay, where do y’all want to park?” Six Nine asked, lowering the volume of the music, looking at Buttons in the rearview to give her the final say. They were about two and a half blocks away from where the Four Horsemen hung out on Mount Street.

“Pull right up on them bitches,” Buttons fired, turning red.

“Nah, let’s rock these bitches.” Nichelle had a plan. “Six, go up Lexington first so we can peep where them bitches chilling at.”

“Then what?” Six Nine questioned.

“Just do it.”

Buttons and them circled Mount Street and found out exactly where the Four Horsemen were sitting.

“Okay, drop me and Yusra off on Baltimore Street. We are going to walk right down Mount Street. Y’all pull up on Fayette Street, right on the corner. Once they see us coming and come toward us, y’all hop out and come up on them from behind.” Nichelle knew her plan would work, but she wanted Yusra with her. She knew Yusra’s little ass could rumble.

“Well, let’s ambush these hookers.” Keisha was ready.

Everybody fell into their own thoughts as Six Nine made her way back around to Baltimore and Mount Street to drop Nichelle and Yusra off.

“Y’all wait until y’all see us park,” Keisha said as Buttons let Yusra out to go up front.

“We about to give these bitches a serious Lucky Charm beat down,” Buttons said just before Six Nine pulled off.

Buttons, Six Nine, and Keisha, who was leaning between the front car seats, watched as Yusra and Nichelle cut the corner and started walking toward the Four Horsemen. All four of them were out there, but to the Charms girls, only Trina and the little bitch were a major threat. However, all of them would go hard.

Got them bitches now, Buttons thought.

Keisha watched the Four Horsemen with the patience of a high school teacher. She was waiting for the moment they would spot Yusra and Nichelle coming from the other end of Mount. "Where these bitches at?" Keisha asked, reaching for her phone. She was about to text Nichelle.

"There they go right there." Six-Nine pointed to the top of the block.

"Come on," Buttons said once Trina noticed Yusra and started heading toward her.

Trina put her crew on point about the good luck. They saw the bait and went after it.

"Here they come," Yusra mumbled to Nichelle without moving her lips.

Keep coming, bitch. Nichelle peeped Buttons and Keisha creeping down Mount Street, and Six Nine wasn't too far behind. *What the fuck is she doing? She's supposed to hold the wheel down.* There was too much going on to focus on Six Nine.

"I see 'em."

Nichelle and Yusra acted like they didn't see Trina and them until they got right up on them.

"Look at these bitches," Trina said.

"Y'all chose the wrong street to walk down," one of Trina's girls followed up.

"Excuse us, please," Yusra said, and it got quiet for a second.

"Bitch, please. Ain't no dick up here." Only Trina was brave enough to challenge Yusra.

"Look, bitch, we don't have time to play games!" Nichelle barked as she watched Buttons and Keisha close in.

"What? Didn't you see how we fucked up that white bitch?" Trina asked.

"I ain't her." Yusra stepped forward.

"You can be. Y'all must think that—"

Pop!

Trina never finished because Buttons hit her so hard that she swallowed the rest of her sentence.

"Didn't I tell you that I'd be back, bitch!" Buttons had put everything she had into that first blow. She tried to end the fight, but Trina had rumbled with the best of them.

"Get that bitch!" Keisha screamed, and it was on.

Buttons was on Trina's ass, but Trina was too much, so Keisha helped her out. Yusra went after the little one she'd always wanted to get her hands on as Nichelle threw the other two around.

A crowd started to form, and Josh was front and center. Trina tried to get a hold of Keisha's hair, but it was too greasy. Five minutes into the brawl, and it was down to Trina and the little bitch; the other two of the Four Horsemen were done. They had matched up with Nichelle, and the fight was over before it started. They were laid by a parked car with no more fight in them. Trina gave her a run for her money, but the truth of the matter was she was no match for two Lucky Charm bitches. Trina's nice, medium-sized, brown titties were out, and some of her hair covered the sidewalk. Once they got Trina and the little bitch down, it was nothing except Timberland boots and Under Armour to the face, head, and body.

"Y'all got 'em!" someone screamed from the crowd. People started to feel sorry for the Four Horsemen.

"Yo, what the fuck! Get the fuck off my sister." Trina's brother pushed through the crowd and hit Keisha like she was a man. "Bitch, back up!" he spun and barked at Buttons before mushing her in the face.

Keisha looked up from the ground, holding her jaw. She was dizzy from the blow.

"I will murder one of you bitches out here!" he threatened, looking at his sister as he made his way toward Buttons. And just as Josh was about to step up, Six Nine pulled out a nickel-plated Snub-Nosed 32 and shot Trina's brother twice in the upper body.

Six Nine saw her ex-boyfriend's face and pulled the trigger again.

"Oh, shit! Six, what the fuck!" Buttons moaned, covering her mouth as blood flowed from Trina's brother's chest. Everybody took off running.

"Let's get the fuck outta here!" Keisha pulled Buttons' arm.

"You shot my brother! Oh my God! Oh my! Please, somebody, help me!" Trina was sitting on the concrete, holding her brother. Her titties and remaining clothes were covered in hers and her brother's blood. "Somebody call an ambulance! Please! He is bleeding to death!"

Buttons heard Trina's cries for help as they ran and jumped back into the car, taking off with Nichelle driving. So much for the plan.

"Oh my God. You shot him. I can't believe you shot him," Keisha said, no longer dizzy. The shots had shaken her out of her daze.

"He should never have put his hands on you. Only a coward of a man hits a woman," Six Nine argued. She would protect her cousin, even if it meant prison. "Don't ever let no nigga put his hands on you. Ever."

Buttons and Yusra were both shaken up. Nichelle had seen niggas get shot down a million times on the Avenue, so it didn't affect her. All Buttons kept thinking about was the look on the guy's face when the shells hit his frame after Six Nine pulled the trigger.

He should've never hit her, Buttons tried to reason with herself. *It was a simple girl fight.*

That night, everybody went their own way with a rehearsed statement in case the police did grab them for the shooting. Buttons was scared, and everybody was worried about her because they had to go over her statement five times before everybody split and went home.

* * * * *

The next week passed faster than usual. The streets were still talking about the shooting. The Lucky Charms were all over Murder Ink, and Buttons and Keisha's names kept being mentioned, but Trina's brother was still in a coma, and the Four Horsemen weren't talking. Buttons dyed her hair back to her natural color—red. She was thinking about going down to Louisiana with her favorite cousin, Chick-a-Dee, until things cooled down.

"Mmmm." Buttons moaned, stretched, wiped the coal from her eyes, and rolled over, dialing Keisha's number. It was early Friday morning.

"Hello? Who else, girl? Yeah. Are you going to school? Me either. I'll be around there. I know. You were right. I ain't going down there. I'ma call my cousin down south today. She's a federal correctional officer."

"Yes. Call Nichelle. Yeah. I'm with it. Tell her just until shit cools down. Okay. No. Whatever. I need the money. I ain't tripping off Yusra. Girl, you crazy. I love you too. Bye." Buttons got up to shower and get dressed. She was going down to the club tonight, anything to take her mind off the shooting. It was still eating her.

"Get that money right because Snow White is in the building," Buttons spoke to herself in the mirror as she held up her white titties and seductively moved her hips from side to side. *Let me go back out on this floor before a bitch goes crazy and starts something I have to finish.* Buttons turned herself on sometimes.

The club started jumping at around eight o'clock. It was Friday night, and checks had been cashed, and hustlers closed shop early. Both crooks and corporate men were out to see some skin. The club atmosphere always did something to Buttons. It made her feel more in control. She could control how far things went. Buttons had popped two E-pills to keep her mind off the shooting. Word from her homegirls at school, Nova and Janette, was that the police had been to the school, looking for members of a girl clique who went by the name Buttons and K-Pay. The police had already knocked on Nichelle's mother's door, so Buttons knew it wouldn't be long.

"Can we get a dance?" a dark-skinned dude asked as Buttons made her way through the tables from her last table dance. Buttons wasn't feeling any pain. All she wanted to do was dance and forget. Her mind was on getting some money.

"Sure, sweetie." Buttons looked at the guy who sat back to watch with his fitted cap on, nursing a drink. She was naked except for four-inch heels, a starkly fishnet, with two matching garter belts full of bills.

"Both of y'all?" Buttons looked at the dark-skinned pretty boy.

"Nah. Just me." The dude slipped a ten-spot into one of Buttons' garter belts.

Buttons started dancing for him. She was putting it on him so good that his dick was hard in no time.

"Look at all that ass." the guy said, lightly tapping her on the butt.

Buttons had her back to the guy. She was playing with her nipples as she looked him in the eyes over her shoulder. "You like that, don't you?" Buttons was talking to him, but turned to look at his friend, the watcher.

"Yeah." The word came out real slow and long. Buttons could tell that the dude behind her was biting his bottom lip as his eyes and mind got trapped in her magic box and hole.

Buttons had been told that whenever she bent over, her asshole seemed to wink.

Buttons started shaking and clapping her ass when Cardi B's 'WAP' song flooded the club's speakers. She watched as the dude's friend licked his fingers and then reached out and played with her nipples for a second.

Oh, he's one of them. Buttons smiled inside. She loved the niggas who tried to act like they just came in the club to support their homies because they always turned out to be the biggest tricks.

"Mmm, mmm, hmm, baby. No touching on the floor." Buttons looked around. She knew that she had him. Buttons had broken the best of them. They came to the club to just look, but before the night was over, she or one of the other girls had them emptying their pockets.

"Look. Let's go to the Showroom, then," the guy spending all the money said, like it was all he wanted to do.

The Showroom, VIP room, Sex room, or whatever someone chose to call it, was located in the rear of the club. It was through a red door and up a set of stairs. There were about eight private rooms where dancers could entertain their customers more privately. It cost fifty dollars to even pass the door with the white question mark painted in the center of it.

"Let's go," Buttons encouraged, feeling good. Fuck it. She was curious anyway. She had never been past the red door. She had heard stories about the things that went on back there. Buttons didn't know what she was going to do when she got back there. *I will give them a real dance.*

Buttons heard that strippers fucked and sucked in the Showrooms, played with themselves for customers, or let them beat their dicks as they danced. You could dance naked in the private rooms. Buttons knew sex was off limits. She also knew that 80 percent of the people who passed through that red door broke the rules. The other 20 percent were people who were in love with a dancer and wanted her away from other customers or were afraid to be seen enjoying a lap dance. There were a few in that 20 percent who just went back there to talk and get to know a dancer better. The dancers called them stalkers.

They entered the fifth room because the first four were occupied. Buttons looked around the room. *So this is it, huh?* Buttons thought that the room would look different. It was a plain room, small in size. It had one long, red, soft leather sofa that could seat about five. In the center of the room was a pole. The blue light did seem brighter.

"Fifty dollars for this?" Buttons was disappointed.

"Nah, sexy, fifty dollars for the privacy," the dude said as he and his man walked in behind Buttons and took a seat on the sofa. They had to adjust to the light. "Come and give me a lap dance." Dude was right to the point. Shit, for fifty dollars and two hours, Buttons jive felt him. Time was money.

The same music that pumped in the club could be heard through a small speaker hanging in the corner of the room. Buttons danced on him like she was fucking him. She rode him, feeling his pipe the whole time.

"Get my peoples." Dude helped Buttons up so she could dance for his man.

"You don't say much, do you?" Buttons asked while using the pole to start. She went up and down on the pole as if she was fucking. Buttons would let the pole rest between the cheeks of her ass, then shake. She was grinding into the pole very slowly.

"Nah," the quiet one replied softly.

"Show us something, Snow White." The other dude was sitting there, dick hard as shit.

Buttons pulled on and removed the fishnet she had on as she made her way seductively to the quiet one. She turned directly in front of him, her big white ass right in his face. Buttons looked over her shoulder with passion in her eyes and started making her ass talk. It was rolling slowly, jumping up and down. By then, Buttons' pussy was so wet that you could literally see the juices running down the insides of her upper legs.

"Mmmmh." The quiet one moaned before slapping Buttons' ass, making it jiggle. He was running his hands up and down Buttons' legs, almost touching her pussy. He went up until his fingers were inches away from the wetness.

Buttons' mind was going wild with thoughts. She was really feeling herself. The more she danced, the wetter and hornier she became. *Damn. I might fuck both of them in here tonight. Shut up, girl. You can't fuck two dudes at once.* Buttons was fighting her sex demons.

"So what do you wanna do, sexy?" the quiet one asked while his hands spread the cheeks of Buttons' ass to get a better view of her pussy and asshole.

Buttons felt her ass spread but didn't respond.

"Talk to me, sexy," the quiet one spoke just before he blew on Buttons' asshole and kissed her pussy lips.

"Can I take you for a ride?"

"I can't." Buttons' mind said 'No', but her body screamed 'Yes'. *His hands are so soft. Damn! He's so soft-spoken.* Buttons spun around and hopped on his lap. "I never—"

"Don't worry."

Buttons was cut off when the quiet one kissed her. She moaned into his mouth, grinding her wet pussy into his crotch, seeking the feeling of his dick. Buttons pushed his hat off his head. *My God!* At that moment, Buttons realized the guy who had her so turned on was, in fact, a woman. Her hair fell into Buttons' hands. She was shocked but, at the same time, became hornier. *I can't do this.*

Buttons got so turned on that she came right there on the spot and cum started running down her thighs. She grabbed the girl by her hair and forcefully kissed her. She mashed her lips into her. Buttons let her hands run wild. She was really a woman. Buttons had seen and felt titties before, but never had she felt the way she felt at that moment. She pushed her hands between the girl's legs and felt the heat. "Mmmh."

"Do you wanna ride?" the woman asked between kisses.

"Yes. God, please. Yes." Buttons moaned.

"Get up."

Buttons followed orders. Once she was up, she watched as the female played on the pole and stripped.

"My husband is just going to watch. You are the customer now." The sound of that only made Buttons hotter.

"Is that understood?" She stepped in front of Buttons and pushed her down onto the sofa. "Lay back, baby."

"Yes." Buttons was sitting at eye level with her pussy. Everything about the woman was sexy to Buttons. *Now I see why men can't control themselves.* Buttons had been curious about women for a long time, but something about this woman made her want to try anything. She felt safe under her command.

"Okay, now listen and listen good." As the woman spoke, she put one of her feet on the edge of the sofa beside Buttons' head, which made her pussy open up in 'Buttons' face. She grabbed Buttons' head with one hand, leaving her husband a good view. If someone were to look in and see them, it would appear as if a guy with long hair was getting his dick sucked.

"Are you ready?"

Buttons was too hypnotized to speak. She couldn't tell if it was the female speaking or, in fact, her pussy. Instead of making herself sound like a fool, Buttons continued to look right at the pussy as she nodded her head yes.

"Good. Now go ahead and eat it." She put pressure on the back of Buttons' head.

Buttons did a head dive. She had always wondered what it would be like to taste another woman's pussy, and there she was. All women had that thought. She thought about how guys always mentioned how good women tasted. She understood now.

Buttons immediately got the hang of it. She ate it like she wanted to be eaten. Now she knew firsthand why men enjoyed eating pussy so much. *Damn. She tastes so lovely.* Buttons' mind was gone. She started thinking about all the times that she'd fantasized about eating Keisha's pussy growing up.

The more the girl moaned and firmly held her head, the more she enjoyed it. *I got my tongue in another woman's pussy.* She was nervous. She thought that she was eating too hard and might hurt her, yet she was envious of the women who got to enjoy eating pussy daily.

"Mmmh, uh. Get my clit."

Buttons felt like she was watching a porno tape starring herself when it was her turn to be eaten. She was climbing the walls of the Showroom. *Oh my God. She's eating my pussy.* Buttons was biting her bottom lip as she watched the chick's husband fuck her from behind while she ate her pussy. It was so soothing, like a hot bath. The first touch of her tongue gave Buttons instant pleasure.

She moaned, twisted, and clawed in ecstasy. The woman was so gentle with her. Chills traveled up and down her spine. Looking at her husband's slow stroke only intensified everything. Buttons could see the moisture on the woman's face, oozing between her fingers and running down the inside of her thighs as the chick held her legs open and worked her clit over. Buttons felt it again. *Oh, God!*

"Stop! I can't come again. I can't. Oh my. It's too much."

* * * * *

Buttons got up the next morning, showered, got dressed, and left the house as if she was going somewhere besides the street corner. She loved sitting out on the block until she was actually sitting out on the block. But hell, that was where the action was. No matter how boring it was, there was always something to see on the block. Keisha was sitting on the steps of the second house from the corner when Buttons cut onto Edmondson Avenue.

"Hey, girl." Buttons took a seat beside Keisha.

"Hey."

"What's up out here?" It was still early.

"Nothing. Ain't nobody out this bitch." Keisha had been sitting on the steps for a minute, just thinking about life. The steps were one of their chill spots.

Buttons just looked around. "I'm getting tired of this shit."

"Tired of what?"

"Sitting around all day, doing nothing with my life."

"I feel you, girl." Keisha felt Buttons. All they ever did was party and bullshit.

They sat in silence for a minute. Buttons wondered how long they would all remain Lucky Charms girls. She thought of school and where she wanted to go in life.

"I'm going back to school Monday." Buttons had a vision. She didn't want to be like most of the girls around the way, hugging the block all her life, switching men, having babies, and partying all day while her mother took care of her kids.

"What about the police?" Keisha jive missed school too, but for a different reason.

"I ain't tripping off them. I can't let them take my education. I got to finish school. I'm in my last year. I don't want to spend my whole life on this block, popping E's and drinking. There's more to life than Edmondson Avenue."

"What are you gonna do after you finish school?"

"I want to start a local business, find a good man, travel, and start a family."

"What the fuck is a good man? You talking about a nigga with some money? Because that's the only thing good about these niggas out here. Every now and then, you might trip on some good dick."

Buttons looked at Keisha like she was crazy. "Nah, I'm talking about a man who challenges me but lets me be myself, a strong man who's not afraid to let me be a woman, one who has my back and knows that I have his no matter what. I want someone to build with, a man who is not scared to struggle." Buttons could picture everything about this man except his face.

"Girl, please. You're really dreaming. I don't know what world you live in. These niggas ain't shit. All they want is some pussy. Think about all these cheating ass, trifling niggas."

Buttons' mind flashed to Ralph. "I ain't talking about these niggas. The city is big, and the world is even bigger. Life is bigger than the Avenue. There are some good men out here. We just got to pick through the trash." Buttons just couldn't believe that there were no good men in the world. Edmondson Avenue and Carey Street maybe, but not the world. She thought of the few men who held shit down by taking care of their kids, being faithful, setting a good example, and working hard. She knew men who covered some of those good qualities, but she drew a blank when trying to think of a man who covered them all. But again, all of the men she knew were chasing hood dreams.

"Show me a good man, and watch me fuck him. Men are weak, girl." Keisha watched as Buttons took in what she was saying.

"I am not saying that he has to be perfect. People make mistakes, Keisha. If he loves you, and you love him, y'all will be okay."

"Men are only out for self, girl. They aren't loyal."

"And what are we?" Buttons was curious to know. She knew that men could be broken, but she also knew, with the right woman, they could also be strengthened.

"We are as strong as our men. We are their reflection. We are both men's strengths and weaknesses."

"Elaborate on that. I don't get it." Buttons was lost.

"Simply put, you can't find a good man. You have to make him. You have to take his few good qualities and build on his bad."

"What?" Buttons looked at Keisha.

"If your man is a good father, encourage that. If he is also a cheater, then you have to keep him pleased."

"Girl, shut up! That's narrow-minded as shit, but I do agree to some extent." Buttons knew that her man wouldn't be perfect. As long as he loved his mother, loved her, and was about teaching her while learning from her, they would be okay.

"The truth don't need no support."

They sat on the steps and talked about life, love, family, education, and men until the Avenue started to liven up.

"Larrrrry!" they both screamed in unison, dragging his name all sexy like.

Larry threw up his balled-up right fist from the other side of the street as he continued to cruise on his bike. "Now that's a man I wouldn't mind making good," Keisha said as she watched Larry riding down the street.

"I bet you would, but you're gonna have to kill Riquel's ass. She doesn't play about that dick." Buttons couldn't help but think about what Nichelle had said about him.

"Yeah. I know. I think that they got married too. That's why his ass been acting all funny."

"Okay, y'all line up in one line! No ones! No fives! And no change! Green and white star-bags out!" a fiend screamed up and down the block to let it be known that shop was open.

Buttons watched as fiend after fiend followed orders. She looked around the grimy streets of West Baltimore. There were kids everywhere. Guys were selling everything from E-pills to weed as if the kids weren't there. *I hope this won't be where life stops for me.* Buttons thought. She couldn't spend the rest of her life like this. This wasn't living.

"One time!" one of the corner lookouts screamed as the police made their way up Edmondson Avenue.

"There go your girl," Keisha said as she looked across the street. "I remember I caught her in the alley sucking some young boy's dick for a blast."

Buttons looked up and saw her nineteen-year-old neighbor haul-assing down the avenue with her h kids by her side and shook her head. The crazy thing was that it didn't look out of place, because it was so normal in the hood.

Chapter 8

Monday morning started off good. Buttons had a good breakfast and was off for school by eight o'clock. Keisha was still skeptical about the police, so she said that if nothing happened to Buttons, she would think about returning right after the New Year. That way, she could start off normally like everybody else after the holidays.

In school, Ms. White informed Buttons that she was behind and needed to do extra homework and class work if she wanted her credits to graduate.

In the cafeteria, Buttons sat with Nova and Janette, as usual.

"Girl, trust me. This nigga is fine with a capital F." Nova was talking about her new boy toy, whom she had booked on the internet. "I'm bringing a picture of him for you tomorrow."

"I can't believe you," Janette had to add her two cents. She and Nova had been beefing about her new man since she found out about him. "You are sitting here talking about this guy like he ain't in prison."

"Don't hate. He will be home in three years. Plus, I was talking to Buttons. So, bye, hater."

Nova rolled her eyes.

"Whatever."

"Anyway, like I was saying, girl. This nigga all cut up and shit. He be telling me all kinds of things in his letters. We talk about everything. I'm going to see him next week,"

Nova confessed. She didn't care what Janette thought about her situation.

"Are you sure that's a good idea?" Buttons was a little concerned.

"Yeah, that's my baby. Plus, I'm going down there with his sister."

"Oh, okay. So what's his name and stuff?" Buttons inquired since it seemed like Nova's mind was made up.

"Reggie. They call him Trigger though. He's from up the Heights. Girl, he's so down to earth. You got to go check out that stillstanding.com shit and holler at one of them niggas, even if it's just to pass time. They got so much on their minds. These niggas out here are full of shit. They ain't trying to have no meeting of the minds. They just wanna fuck! They think that a relationship is about sex. Dick can only hold a bitch hostage for so long."

Laughing, Buttons said, "I might check it out." Buttons' mother had just gotten internet access. "Are men really that bad?"

"Yes," Nova quickly replied. "I mean, I want more than sex. Look at these bum ass niggas in here. These niggas ain't shit."

I keep hearing that, Buttons thought for a second as she took a look around. "Yeah, some of them need to tighten up."

"And this is coming from two dizzy ass chicks chasing prison love, a bunch of homo thugs, at that." Janette couldn't believe them. They were crazy in her eyes. "Who the fuck picked a locked-up nigga over a free one? Damn fools. That was who."

"Shut up. Damn! You don't know shit. Stop passing judgment on something you know nothing about." Nova didn't like when people did that.

"All I'm saying is that he is locked up. Why would anybody want a man in jail when they could have a free one?" Janette just couldn't understand.

"Who is going to allow themselves to keep getting treated like shit? I mean, if it's real, it's real. Fuck where he's at. How is he treating you? I mean, the last time I checked, your man wasn't on his job. You even said it yourself. His big, clown ass can't even fuck."

Janette stared at her.

"And what about your cousin? The one you always talking about? Is he a homo?"

"Don't even play." Janette wasn't about to play that game. "You know what I mean."

"You did say it like all men in prison were faggies," Buttons added her two cents.

"I ain't saying *all*, just a lot. My cousin is not one of them."

"Neither is my man. Anyway, that's a myth, but you would have to have a relationship with a real man in prison to know that and notice that I said *man*," Nova stated matter-of-factly. She knew that the faggie thing about prison, along with the bread and water thing, were just two of the bigger misconceptions about prison.

"You keep watching *OZ* and them other dumb ass prison shows, and you won't have a clue. Producers will play anything that sells, just like the news will say anything to turn the people against you."

"Okay, girl, damn! My bad. I didn't mean it the way you're taking it." Janette knew that most of her prison information came by rumors or prison shows, so she decided to let it go. "So Buttons, what's with the red hair?"

"I wanted a new look, but I'm dying it back blonde this weekend."

Nova and Janette looked at each other and laughed. "You been really getting wild, Ms. Bonnie."

"Huh?" Buttons didn't catch what Janette said.

"Are you going to tell us what happened or keep us in limbo?" Nova asked.

"Tell you about what?" Buttons hoped she wasn't talking about the shooting.

"Come on now. The shooting, bitch!" Nova said, like Buttons was playing.

"Don't believe everything you hear." Buttons started to feel uncomfortable.

"Did you really shoot them?" Janette asked. She had to know. Buttons didn't look like a killer to her.

"Them?" Buttons eyed her. *Who the fuck is them?*

"Yeah, Trina and her brother," Nova replied.

Damn! I ain't even know Trina got hit. She didn't look shot to me. Buttons got up, grabbed her food tray, and walked away from the table. *Why the fuck does everybody keep watching me?* People had been watching her all day, moving out of her way in the hallways and bathroom. It kind of made Buttons nervous. She looked around as she made her way out of the cafeteria after disposing of her leftover food and racking her tray.

Buttons had no idea that the shooting had given her some real street credit, and all of her fellow students were watching her out of fear, curiosity, admiration, and hate. Some who heard the Trina getting shot story felt like Buttons had done them a favor. Trina and the Four Horsemen had a lot of victims' blood under their Timberland boots.

* * * * *

Buttons knew she was going to have to buckle down if she wanted to finish the school semester. With extra work each period and some extra homework, she knew she could bring her grades back up. She was only a few weeks behind.

"Ms. Howard, I will not accept any more unexcused absences from you. You are a very smart young lady with a bright future ahead of you, but you will let that slip away if you don't apply yourself," Buttons' third-period science teacher was saying.

Fake motherfucker! Buttons knew that he was just talking, putting on a show for himself. He didn't give a flying fuck one way or another. He slept through the whole period and had the nerve to be running his mouth, knowing he only came to work for the money.

"Bli, bli, bli, bli, bli… Is that understood?"

"Yes." Buttons didn't hear half of the shit he said.

Buttons made her way to the last period. She felt good about coming back. She had truly missed school. Although it got on her nerves at times, she knew she had to finish if she wanted to get anywhere in life. Education was the key to life in Buttons' mind. She understood that, in order to survive in the real world, she would need to be educated. People loved taking advantage of less educated people; the strong preyed on the weak.

"Good afternoon, class," the teacher said once all of her students were seated and had settled down.

"Good afternoon!" the class replied in unison.

After roll call, the teacher passed out a three-question pop quiz. "Okay, class, let's get started."

Buttons kept watching the clock. Damn. *Why does shit go slow when you close in on the end?* Buttons loved school, but like any other kid, she felt like when it was time to go, it was time to go. Buttons was inside her own thoughts when the final school bell rang. Everybody started moving at once. The bell was like a long-awaited phone call from a loved one.

"Okay class, drop your quizzes on my desk on your way out. They will be graded and returned," the teacher spoke as the kids rushed to exit the class.

Look at them. Can't get them to school and can't keep them there. Buttons watched as about two other students wrote anything on the third quiz question. The bell had sounded, and it was time to go. Nothing else mattered.

Buttons was one of the last to exit the classroom. "Hello, there."

Buttons turned and noticed the guy Montego leaning on the lockers just outside the classroom. *Not again. What the fuck is he? A stalker or something?*

"Hi." Buttons kept moving. She didn't feel like it today.

"Can I have a minute, Brittany?" he asked.

Not wanting to be rude, Buttons stopped and turned to face him. "Please call me Buttons."

"I like Brittany better," he replied, licking his lips.

Buttons rolled her eyes. "Your minute has started." At that moment, Buttons realized what the crazy ass, black nigga had on. *Oh my God! No, he doesn't have on a fishnet tank top, old ass, cut-off True Religion jean shorts, dress socks, and sandals.*

"Let me take you out to the movies or something." Montego had loose threads hanging from his shorts and all.

He couldn't be serious. He had to be joking. "No, boy! I mean, I got a boyfriend." Buttons looked at him like he was crazy. She couldn't believe what he had on. He couldn't think that shit was cool.

"What is that man got to do with me?" He looked at her as if she was supposed to laugh. "Wooooo. Nern talkin' 'bout?"

"What?" Buttons didn't know what the hell he was talking about. "Look, your minute is up." She stepped off quickly. *Was that a line? He must have his own language.* Buttons knew it was some weak-game-having niggas, but damn. Ol' boy took the cake.

"I'll see you around!" he yelled behind her.

Child, please. Buttons never responded, nor did she look back. She figured he must've been one of the Jamaicans her girls warned her about, the ones you said hi to or looked at a second too long, and they thought y'all were married. *I hope I don't have to get him fucked up.*

Buttons got home and did some extra homework, took a shower, and tried to relax. "Are you hungry, Brittany?" Her mother cracked her bedroom door and peeped in.

Buttons was lying across the bed in her panties and bra. "Yes."

"Put something on and come on down and get you something to eat." Jessica pulled the door closed.

Jessica had cooked a nice baked chicken dinner. Leroy sat beside Buttons at the small, square kitchen table. One side was pushed up against the wall, leaving room to seat only three people.

"So how was school?" Jessica asked as she put food on both Leroy's and Buttons' plates.

"It was fine." Buttons watched as Leroy rubbed her mother's ass as if she wasn't there. He was squeezing handfuls and making it shake.

"Quit it, Leroy." Jessica smiled and popped his hand, but she felt like a schoolgirl.

"Damn, baby. I can't help myself around your fine ass." Leroy looked at Buttons.

Negro, please! Buttons rolled her eyes. All through dinner, Buttons felt Leroy's nasty ass hand rubbing her thighs. He got so bold a few times that he actually moved his hand up to her pussy. Buttons couldn't help but close her eyes at the sensation. Her mother was sitting directly across from her.

Buttons kept looking at her mother as she talked about her day at work. When Jessica excused herself to use the bathroom, Leroy jumped up and stood over Buttons. He forced her back down in her chair when she tried to get up, trapping her.

"Don't play."

Buttons looked nervously toward the steps.

"I like that red hair. I bet your little draws on fire." Leroy unzipped his jeans.

"Leroy, don't." Buttons was scared her mother wasn't that far. "Please." She heard her mother moving around upstairs.

"Daddy, bitch!" Leroy pulled his hard dick out and started rubbing it all over her face.

Buttons was breathing extra hard and wiping around her mouth when Jessica entered the kitchen.

"Brittany, are you okay?" Jessica heard her daughter slightly choking and gagging.

"Yeah," Buttons replied as little choking tears rolled from her eyes.

"Ye-yeah. My food went down the wrong pipe." Buttons could feel the thick, sticky feeling in her throat as she spoke. It was like a little bubble, making it hard to breathe.

"Drink some water." Jessica handed her a glass of water.

"You should stop eating so fast," Leroy said from his seat with a little smirk on his face.

"Brittany, I have told you that you need to stop eating so fast." Jessica looked at her. "Are you sure you are okay?"

"I'm okay, Ma." Buttons felt her throat clear with the water. "It was just a little food."

"Little?" Leroy had to catch himself. "I saw all that chicken in your mouth."

"Brittany, what did I tell you about that?" Jessica sat down. "Take your time when you eat. You don't have to rush; it ain't going nowhere. She's picking up those bad habits from hanging in those streets."

"Sorry, Ma." Buttons looked at her. *She's so damn dumb. I will be moving soon. You can believe that.*

"I will slow down next time."

"Good," Jessica said. "Now, finish up." Jessica eyed Leroy.

Buttons knew that Jessica's world was nothing like hers. That night, she listened as Leroy fucked the dog shit out of her mother. She could hear the moans and skin slapping. When she heard her mother begging for mercy, she knew it only meant one thing. Leroy was fucking her mother in the ass. Buttons prayed for Leroy's death before drifting off to sleep.

* * * * *

The next morning in school, Buttons' mind was everywhere but school, though she managed to complete her class work. She had talked to Keisha at about four o'clock in the morning. Buttons' mind was on Trina, the ringleader of the Four Horsemen's crew. They had crossed paths just before second period without incident, which was cool with Buttons. She wasn't looking for any trouble, but she wouldn't duck if it came her way.

"Look at my baby!" Nova said, handing Buttons a photo of her new locked-up friend named Reggie. He had on some white-on-white high-top Nike flights and a prison-issued navy-blue uniform that had the letters D.O.C. written on the right leg.

"So he's a Libra, huh? October seventh is my cousin birthday too." Buttons was looking at the older dude. She knew that was what she needed, an older dude who was real and could teach her. "So, he good people?"

"Yes, girl. That's my baby. And like I told you, his sister, Adrienne, is cool as shit too." Nova was pumped up, and Buttons was happy for her.

Janette just sat back and rolled her eyes.

"Richardson! I might know some of his family." Buttons read the last name on the back of the photo.

"Shit, you might."

They went on to talk about the website, why Reggie was locked up, and a lot of other things.

"Yeah, I might check it out just to look at some hard bodies," Buttons said, thinking of all the eye candy she might see. She knew that hard bodies and prison were connected like day and night.

"Watch some of the guys you see on there. They're damn near naked. Shit, I had a hard time picking just one." They all busted out laughing at Nova's statement. "Girl, I was about to touch myself."

"Mmmh, stillstanding.com, right?" Buttons asked to be sure.

"Yes, stillstanding.com, girl," Nova responded just as the lunch bell rang.

Buttons got home early from school and was glad to find the house empty. After doing her homework, Buttons called and talked to Keisha for a few minutes.

"Damn! It's boring as shit!" Buttons said to herself after hanging up the phone. *What the fuck am I going to do? I don't feel like going outside. My homework is done. Shit!* Buttons looked around. *I should watch a movie. Nah. Oh yeah. I'm go play on that website shit. What's the name again? Standingup.com? Nah. Standingstill.com? Fuck. That ain't it.* The name was on the tip of Buttons' tongue. "Got it. Stillstanding. Yeah, that's it." She walked to the front room where the computer her mother had just got was located.

It took Buttons every bit of thirty minutes to get online. She was thankful for her basic computer class in school. She had never seen so many real bad boys in one place. She was seeing body after body—white boys, blacks, and all other races in between. It was fun, reading what they had to say. Some were talking about love, some about fun, and others, both.

"Oh my God! He's a freak!" Buttons was reading the end of some guy's ad.

Buttons turned the computer off after about two hours of profile reading. The site was still relatively new, and according to the ad count at the beginning, there were only 2,637 ads posted. Buttons was sure it was because of the things you had to go through to post your ad. She had passed maybe five hundred ads, most of which she simply zoomed through. The only time she actually read an ad in its entirety was when she saw something that intrigued her. She looked for age, sentences, photos, and zodiac signs. Buttons felt like she was in a candy store.

Buttons had read up on zodiac signs in the past, so she wanted an Aquarian or a Sagittarius. She knew both of their negative and positive traits. Buttons knew that both Aquarius and Sagittarius were freaks and unselfish. She read that there was no limit to what Aquarius and Sagittarius would do in a relationship.

Buttons was thinking about what she read. Aquarians were ahead of their time with their outlook on life. They thought about what they would be doing in five years, while most people couldn't even think about what they would do next week. And Buttons, she was always looking to the future. Both signs were independent. Buttons' mind was running wild. She was a flirt, and Aquarians weren't insecure; that was a plus, and they both loved sex. Buttons cut the computer off and went to make herself something to eat.

"Brittany!" Jessica spoke, walking into the kitchen with her hands full of paperwork.

It wasn't a good day for her. Her boss had been on her back all day. Jumping down her throat about any little mistake.

"Hi, Ma," Buttons said and continued to eat her cheese hot dogs.

"Where's Leroy?" Jessica asked.

"I don't know. He ain't been here all day." Buttons looked at her mother and knew she could do so much better. At that moment, the front door opened and closed.

"Jessica!"

"Speaking of the devil."

"Watch your mouth." Jessica eyed her.

Leroy didn't enter the kitchen; he just stood in the doorway. They could tell that he was drunk. "Hey, baby!" Leroy grabbed his dick and squeezed it.

"Leroy!" Jessica looked at Buttons. She could smell the liquor. "Where have you been? You were supposed to pick me up from work, Leroy."

"Bitch, don't question me. Who the fuck is you? That's all y'all bitches' problem. Don't know when to shut the fuck up. I got something you can do with that mouth of yours." Leroy shook his dick at her.

Jessica looked at him like he was crazy. She knew he had to see her daughter sitting right there. "Leroy, don't disrespect my daughter like that. Are you crazy?" Jessica barked.

Buttons could hear her mother's broken spirit behind the strong words.

"Bitch, she know the deal up in here. I slang the pipe around here!" Leroy was really feeling himself. Fuck that little bitch! "Now come 'ere."

Jessica walked to him. She didn't want to argue with him. Leroy grabbed her hair and forced his tongue in her mouth. He took his other hand and squeezed Jessica's ass cheeks. Her skirt came up, revealing the lower part of her white ass cheeks. One side of her panties was bunched up into her ass crack. Buttons couldn't believe how weak her mother was for this nigga.

"Brittany, go to your room," Jessica broke the kiss to say.

Buttons just eyed her mother and got up. *You are pathetic. I will never be like you.* Buttons rolled her eyes and left.

"Why you gotta disrespect me in front of my daughter, Leroy?" Buttons heard her mother ask in a whisper just as she left the room, thinking she couldn't hear.

"That little bitch grown. Besides, you act like you ain't my bitch." Buttons paused outside the kitchen doorway. Surely, her mother would defend her honor.

"Yes, Leroy, I am your bitch."

Buttons' heart broke.

"And you want this dick, don't you, white girl?"

Buttons felt like she didn't have a mother.

"Yes."

"Say it then, slut."

"I want that dick."

"Go get it then…"

Buttons fled to her room as tears rolled from her eyes. *I got to get out of here.*

After some time, Buttons could hear them in the kitchen. *My mother is a fucking slut. She let this sucker do anything. I'm starting to wonder if she knows he be raping me.*

Buttons' next step was to move. That shit was not right. Buttons wanted to call Keisha, but she wouldn't understand. *What about Yusra? Damn, I need someone to talk to, someone who will just listen.* She knew that she had to get it out because it was killing her inside. She laid down to rest her nerves.

Buttons woke up around one in the morning and couldn't go back to sleep, so she started writing a letter to someone. Who? It didn't matter; she just left the name blank. She gave a confessional rundown of her life and the things she had endured. Some things, she left out. She described herself, her likes and dislikes, strengths and weaknesses. She talked about her friends, mother, and evil stepfather. It took almost an hour to finish, but Buttons had to admit that she felt so much better. It was like a weight off her shoulder. Still, she knew she would feel much better if someone could read her thoughts, but it was cool. Buttons remembered reading somewhere that writing was therapeutic.

Buttons jumped out of bed as an idea hit her. That was it. She slipped her feet into her slippers.

"This is him. This is the one." Buttons looked at the man standing on a prison basketball court on the computer screen. "Yeah, this is him." She had been sitting at the computer, reading ads for less than an hour when she found what she was looking for. His ad was so simple yet so real. *I hope he doesn't think I'm hard up.*

I mean, I ain't looking for no husband, just a friend to trade thoughts with. She wasn't even sure if she was going to send a real photo of herself. *Shit! I might send him a picture of my mother.*

Buttons started laughing, not sure if she would really mail the letter, but there was something in his eyes that said, “Trust me,” and that alone was working in his favor.

Chapter 9

"Zix, zeven, zate, zine, zen." Rayven finished his fifteenth set of push-ups. He was doing twenty sets of ten push-ups and twenty back arms. Rayven was more than halfway through his lock-up time.

When Rayven went in front of the hearing officer for the assault and weapon charge, he received 150 days on lockup and one year's loss of his visitation rights. He made out because he hadn't had a serious infraction since going to the supermax almost five years prior. All he did on lockup was read, write, study law, work out, and listen.

Rayven had learned a long time ago that it was more to being a so-called gangsta than just going hard and putting in work. Putting in work was only 30 percent of being a man or so-called gangsta. One had to be educated, fast on their feet, and passive as well as aggressive, amongst other things. Mind, body, and soul all played a part in being a man, and Rayven had mastered that.

The other guys on lockup were his TV. He could catch drama, action, suspense, etcetera, all on the tier. Rayven sat back, listened, and tripped off how dudes tried to make up reasons to be weak and excuses to fuck with rats. Moon made sure he was good by bringing him books, little goodies, and making phone calls for him. The internet still hadn't proven fruitful. Rayven promised that the next time some dude talked about how he'd gotten twenty hits, he would call him out on it.

"Twenty, one, two, three, four, five…" Rayven was sweating hard as shit. The sit-ups had his stomach on fire. It was still worth it though. He lifted the wet T-shirt up to look at his rock-hard stomach. *Niggas ain't getting money like me.* He took a breath. *Come on, Slim. Let's earn this bird bath.* Rayven pulled his feet from under the cell door, got up, and walked over to the bunk to do his back arms. *No pain, no gain, baby!* "One, two, three, four… zeven."

"Rayven!"

Rayven looked up to see Moon looking into the cell door glass.

"Let me finish this set." He continued. "… zineteen, zunny." He stood up, took a few breaths. and walked to the door. "What's up, dug?"

"Ain't shit. I talked to One Love and Mini-Me last night." Moon referred to Rayven's mother and daughter.

"How they doing?" He was still jive out of breath.

Rayven's mother was his super power, and his daughter was his kryptonite. Although he didn't always say it or even act like it at times, they were his everything.

"They're good. Your mother did say that you need to get on your daughter though. She ain't say why. She just said you would know," Moon said. "And Ms. Hopskins still holding the cell.

I would know? Man, Mini-Me little ass better not be acting up again. "I'm on it," Rayven replied. "And tell Ms. Hopskins that I said thank you."

"I think she's sweet on you," Moon suggested.

"Most women are." Rayven smiled, feeding right into it.

"Man, I was joking. Ms. Hopskins doesn't want your old ass."

They kicked it for a minute. Moon updated Rayven on what was going on in the jail, all the new dudes that came in, and who was the latest person to get robbed, fucked up, slapped out, or chopped down. Then Moon left to go feed up for lunch.

Rayven only came out of the cell for showers. The doors were only open Monday through Friday. One week, recreation fell on Monday, Wednesday, and Friday, while showers fell on Tuesday and Thursday. The next week, it would switch, and so on and so on. Rayven didn't have a problem living with himself. A lot of dudes couldn't spend twenty-four hours a day in a cell alone. They'd go crazy for many reasons. They couldn't live with themselves, they couldn't live with the crimes, or they couldn't live without something or someone. Guys would lose their minds and take their own lives behind the cell door.

Rayven wasn't one of them. Too much time to think did one of two things—revealed the weak and the strong. Rayven felt the sorriest for the so-called thugs behind the 24-hour-a-day lockdown door who couldn't read or write. He remembered a time when he was one of them. Growing into a man, he knew it was about more than just going hard and putting in work. He was what they called a thug, a gangsta, the truth, and a soldier, all mixed in one. Rayven was twice the G that he appeared to be. What made him all of those things was the fact that he was intelligent, standup, honorable, respectable, and go hard, among other things.

Rayven gave his best to being a good father, friend, son, etcetera, even in prison. He knew he wasn't perfect. He was just a man who stood behind all of his actions, and he believed in something greater than himself. Rayven was known as a triple threat amongst men. He was educated and thorough, with nothing to lose besides some more hair.

"Yo, they might give me a time cut because they need some space." Rayven was sitting on the floor at the back of the cell, talking to his neighbor and playing chess through the vent that traveled through all the cells. They sounded as if they were in the same cell together. Whenever rookie COs came through, they always assumed the prisoners were talking to themselves, not knowing any better. "Lady knight, pawn four."

"I hope they do let you off early, but you know men don't get too many breaks," the old head said.

"Man knight to man bishop, three."

Rayven wished some of the good men could go out with him. He was tired of watching the administration take away the things a lot of older men, himself included, had fought to get. In his eyes, the new breed of prisoners was mostly weak. It wasn't really an age thing; niggas just weren't cut like they used to be.

"I'm ready to get up off lock." Rayven could handle the door. It was the dudes that he was tired of. All they did was talk all day. "Last night I wanted to tell the kid in eighteen to read a book or something."

"I feel you." He knew late nights were the best time to study because everybody was asleep, and the tier was usually quiet.

"I just ain't want to be disrespectful." Rayven knew that only cowards started trouble. Men usually finished it. He treated all men fairly, never knowing when they might be of some help. He never burned bridges unless he was certain he wouldn't have to cross them again. "Man rook, pawn three."

"Yeah, Slim, everything is watered down these days. It's a new day. These niggas done forgot who the enemy is. They disrespect the female officers but respect the male ones. They say women are weak, but they forget that women are a reflection of men and the environment."

He had to laugh. "I see what you're trying to do. Move my man pawn to four."

"Okay." Rayven saw two moves ahead. "These kids are lames. The women COs are playing them, starting wars and shit."

He could understand why they never got any play. Women gravitated to strength. Rayven listened to niggas talking out of the door about female officers who liked to watch dick, what they talked about with them, etcetera. It was no secret that women loved dick, just like men loved pussy. The problem was the lames. They couldn't hold water, so why would they get chosen? The women knew that if they talked about nothing, they would go off about something.

"Okay, Slick. Let's do this. Move my lady to my man rook five. Check."

"Oh, yeah? You know I ain't going for that."

"Oh, yeah? Watch my next move." Rayven smiled, although he couldn't see his opponent's face.

After Moon finished feeding up, he stopped and yelled at Rayven before he left for the day.

Rayven lay back in his own thoughts. He knew what it was like to wake up fucked up. Every now and then, it would be one of those days where no matter what he did, it was just a fucked up day. A life bid could do that.

I got to get up out of this joint. Rayven got up, flipped his mattress back, and pulled out his legal shit: transcripts, motions, and case law. Prison was for the birds. Niggas thought the shit was cool. *But wasn't nothing cool about niggas living to die.* All the niggas in prison had gotten caught. What the fuck was cool about that? Some days were worse than others.

This shit got to be retroactive. Rayven was looking at the 2000-term Frank C. Lance's first-degree murder case, where Lance and his co-defendant, Player, were convicted on mere flagrant testimony. The conviction was later overturned and nullified.

Rayven was going over his notes and pro se motions. *Smallwood statements are ambiguous as shit! How the hell did they find me guilty?* His only rational thought was that maybe the state's misconduct had inspired an impression of guilt. *If they think I'm about to lay down on this shit, they got another thing coming. This is not the last chapter of my life. They can believe that.*

* * * * *

Buttons waited a few days before mailing off the letter. She was sure he would receive it within the week. She got up early as usual for school, took a long, hot shower, used the bathroom, brushed her teeth, and went to fix herself a bowl of cereal. It was Cap'n Crunch that day.

Damn! "Hello?" *Always when I am almost out the door.* Buttons turned back around. "Buttons!" She instantly recognized Keisha's voice.

"Hey, girl." Buttons perked up. "I was on my way out the door."

"Girl, they locked my cousin up!"

"What?"

"They just locked Six Nine up. Police ran all up in my aunt's house, talking about attempted murder charges and shit."

"Attempted murder? On who?"

"Trina's brother."

Buttons could hear tears in Keisha's voice. She couldn't speak for a few seconds. It was always something. "When did this happen?"

"This morning. The police came over here, too, but I was at the store."

Buttons was really starting to get scared now. "What about the gun?"

"My brother took it."

"You want me to come over there?"

"Nah. Let me find out what's going on first."

"How would they know she did it?" Buttons questioned curiously.

"She ain't do shit!" Keisha fired. "Those Four Horsemen bitches snitching."

"Listen. We will talk when I get over there after school. Okay?" Buttons wondered what that meant for the rest of them.

"Okay. Love you, girl."

"I love you too." Buttons hung up. *Oh my God! Six Nine is in jail for life.* Buttons didn't know anything about the system. Flashbacks of the shooting started playing in her head again.

In school, Buttons was zoning. By third period, she had used the bathroom twice. Buttons couldn't handle that shit. She skipped lunch and impatiently waited for the school day to come to an end.

"Ms. Howard, can I please have a word with you outside?" Buttons' fourth-period teacher asked, coming into the classroom.

"Huh?" Buttons was still zoning. "What?"

"I need to speak with you. Please follow me outside." The teacher walked toward the door.

Buttons appeared to be somewhere else. *What the fuck does this motherfucka want?* Buttons got up and made her way to the door.

"Yes?" Buttons said, stepping out into the hallway, looking around. She instantly knew something wasn't right.

"Ms. Howard, these gentlemen need to speak with you." The teacher turned and reentered the classroom, leaving Buttons with two detectives and a plain-clothes Baltimore City police officer. She didn't even give her a chance to respond.

"Brittany Howard, right?" The heavy-set plain clothes officer asked.

"Yes," Buttons admitted

"Is Ms. Jessica Howard your mother?" the heavy-set uniformed officer continued.

"Yes." Buttons' stomach started turning. She already wasn't feeling good. "Has something happened to my mother?" As much as she hated her mother at times and wished for her death, she knew that if something happened to her, she would go off. She knew everyone only got one mother.

Deciding not to play games with her emotions and be direct, he answered with a simple "No."

"What is this about then?" Buttons' heart was still pounding, but she was glad for the news.

"We need you to come downtown for questioning," the black male detective informed.

"Questioning?" Buttons started backing away from them. She was lost.

"Yes. We have information placing you on the scene of a crime."

"You are looking at attempted murder charges," the other cute, female detective added, working her case-cracking games.

"I ain't shoot nobody!" Buttons barked.

"We never said you did." A smile spread across the detectives' faces. "Let's just take a ride downtown."

As they walked through the school hallways, students were making comments like,

"That's her right there."

"That bitch is crazy."

"That's what she get for trying to be black."

"That bitch got mad bodies."

"Oh, shit! The detectives got her."

"They got your bad ass now!"

Students were watching as Buttons was escorted out of the school building by the three officers to an unmarked car.

In the car, Buttons was scared to death. They rode in silence. *I can't go to jail.* She started thinking about what they had talked about, saying if they were ever picked up. These people weren't dumb. *Why would they grab me? I ain't do shit!* Buttons looked out the window, but for some reason, she couldn't see anything.

Before long, they were pulling into a closed-in parking lot. The men got out and had to open the back door for Buttons.

"This way, Ms. Howard."

Buttons followed them through some doors and onto an elevator. The cute female detective pushed button number six. They got off on what Buttons assumed was the sixth floor, walked through the dimly lit hall, and passed several doors, some open and some closed. Inside one of the open rooms, Buttons could see a woman sitting at a steel table being interrogated by two detectives. One of the two men inside pushed the door closed but not before she recognized that it was one of her friends as they began crying before putting their head down.

I knew this would happen! What the fuck was I thinking? Now all of us are going to jail. Buttons wondered which room held her other girls.

"Have a seat," the cute female detective said after they entered an identical room to the one her girl was sitting in.

"I am Detective Gibson," the cute female detective spoke first. "And this here is my partner, Detective Baker." She nodded toward the half-slick, black detective.

"I ain't do nothing." Buttons started to cry.

"Listen, little girl. You are in a lot of trouble. Your friends have put the blame on you, the only white girl. What did you think they would do? We also have other witnesses." The games had begun.

"You are facing a life sentence. You don't want to know what they do to pretty little white girls like you in prison," Detective Gibson said.

"But I ain't do nothing." Buttons was noticeably shaken.

"Don't play with me, young lady!" Detective Baker leaned over the table until his nose was touching Buttons'. It almost looked as if he would kiss her. Both of his hands were flat on the cold, steel table. "We know you pulled the trigger, Ms. Howard."

"Ease up, Baker." Detective Gibson pulled her partner back as if she was on Buttons' side. It was the good cop, bad cop tactic. "Let me talk to her alone."

"Listen, Brittany," the detective said softly as soon as Detective Baker was out of the room. "You are the same age as my little sister. These girls are putting all the weight on you. I don't want to see you go to jail. Your teachers said you are a bright student, but listen. You gotta help me out here."

"What is it you want?"

"The truth. The simple truth."

"Okay." Buttons sat up. "We were over at Keisha's house earlier."

"Who?"

"Me, Keisha, and Six Nine…"

"Hold on just a sec," Detective Gibson turned and signaled for her partner. "Bring in the recorder please."

At that moment, Buttons realized that it was a two-way mirror to the left. *Oh, these motherfuckas are in there watching me.*

Detective Baker entered the room, carrying a tape recorder. He set it in the middle of the steel table and pressed the record button.

"Ms. Howard, before we begin, I'll have you state your full name and today's date for the record. Then, I'll read you your rights," Detective Gibson explained.

Gibson began reading Buttons her memorandum of rights. "You have the right to an attorney. If you can't…" Gibson was reading line for line. "Do you understand those rights?"

"Yes."

Detective Baker went through the process of making sure the recording was legal. He stated his full name, date, time, and title, named his partner as the witness, and ran down the statement of facts.

"Do you know any of these women?" Detective Gibson asked, spreading photos across the table.

"Yes." Buttons looked at the photographs of the Four Horsemen. "I know all of them."

"Okay. Why don't you start from the beginning and tell us how the day in question played out?" Detective Gibson said after Detective Baker whispered something in his ear.

"Like I said, we were over Keis's house and–"

"Keis?" Detective Gibson repeated, cutting her off.

"Yeah, Keis, as in Keisha," Buttons snapped as if they should know.

"Oh. Okay, continue."

"It was early. Nichelle called up to the house and said we were going out." Buttons started crying. She couldn't remember all that she was supposed to say.

"Then what?" Detective Baker was on the edge of his seat.

Six Nine's words echoed in Buttons' head. "*If you get spooked and can't remember the lick, just shut up. Ask for a lawyer, and ride it out. Don't force it. No statement is better than a fucked up one.*"

"I want a lawyer." Buttons smiled to herself now. She felt more in control. Six Nine's words were still running in her head. "*You can always make a statement, but you can't always take one back.*"

"You are going away for a long time, young lady." Detective Baker stopped the recorder and stood up with an attitude. "I will personally see to it."

"Damn! We were just cool a minute ago," Buttons reminded.

Both detectives left Buttons in the room alone. She knew from her girls that they were trying to spook her. *If they got them, why do they need me?* Buttons rationalized.

The room was starting to get cold to Buttons as she sat there alone and did as Six Nine had directed her to do—rode it out.

* * * * *

Knock, knock!

"Yo!" Rayven was lying back on his bed, head propped up on a homemade pillow. He was holding a freak novel in his left hand as he slowly stroked his petrolatum-greased dick while reading. The name of the book was *The Prison Guard's Wife*.

"Mail, Lewis," a female CO said. She couldn't see into the cell because Rayven had the window on the door covered with his lock-up jumpsuit.

"Slide it under." Rayven wasn't trying to move.

Always when a nigga about to nut.

Rayven could hear when the officer pushed the mail under the door. "You better uncover this window, Lewis."

"I'm using the bathroom."

"Whatever. Just have it uncovered when I do my rounds for count." She knew he was lying. *You're probably in there sharpening one of them knives or something.*

Rayven went back to reading and stroking.

"Your man's ain't this big, is it?" Gary asked the counselor as he let his snake dangle in her face. They were inside the counselor's office, supposedly taking care of legal business.

"No." She swallowed. Her husband, Sergeant Briggs, had escorted Gary to her office and was still waiting just outside the door.

"Touch it," Gary spoke, looking down at the fine ass snow bunny from the UK, who was his counselor and forbidden fruit.

Counselor Lisa Briggs couldn't help herself when it came to Gary. That was the second time that week, and it was only Wednesday. She reached up and grabbed his black snake.

"Gary, please. He's right outside," Lisa pleaded, and Gary loved the sound of her accent.

"So?" He knew the circumstances excited her as much as they did him. "You know what time it is…"

Rayven started beating off extra fast as he continued to read.

"That's right, baby. Just like that… Oh, bitch! Take the whole thing…" Gary could feel the tightness of the counselor's throat. It felt so soft as her tonsils stroked the top of his dick like a miniature tongue as he forced his way down into her chest. "Aha."

After taking a bird bath in the sink, Rayven picked up his mail. He didn't recognize the name but figured it had to be someone he knew. The return address was from his old hood. Once he opened the letter, he found a photo of four females who appeared to be no more than twenty. He looked at the back, and the date said it was a recent photo. It looked like there was a party going on in the background.

Damn! These little young girls bad! There were no names on the picture. Rayven looked at the four girls. One of them almost looked white. If it wasn't for her hairdo and gear, Rayven would have tagged her as a white girl. He put the photo down and started reading the letter.

Oh, shit! This is an internet hit. Rayven smiled. He had lucked up.

Damn, shorty! Rayven was still reading. "That's crazy." He didn't know what to think as he read on. "Wow," was all that he could say when he finished reading, he didn't know if the chick was crazy or real for telling him all of that personal shit in a first letter. "She was forward as shit."

Rayven decided to write Buttons back that night. It was something about her that had him intrigued, wanting to know more. The fact that she lived near his old stomping grounds didn't hurt. He wanted to know who her people were and why she didn't know him. He knew she was like eight when he left the streets, but still, everybody knew him around the Avenue. He was a legend.

Rayven went back at her with realness, not game. He touched on everything she touched on and answered all her questions. He pitched her a few ideas and told her that if she would keep it street, he would love to exchange thoughts. At the end of the letter, before signing off sincerely, he asked her if she had any idea what the 'Cinderella Complex' was.

He put the letter in the door for the midnight officer to pick up.

After brushing his teeth and doing his nightly routine pushups, Rayven got in bed and read a little bit of *Before the Mayflower*, hit the light, and laid in the dark with his own thoughts. *Damn. I got to win my post.* Life was passing him by. Over ten years and still no break. He was still trapped off, looking at magazines of air-brushed women, perfect houses, listening to the radio, and wishing it were him. He watched the phony continue to have luck, but the worst was having to have faith in the same system that placed him where he was.

Rayven just laid there, looking at the back of his eyelids. He was now mad at Smallwood for being weak, the streets for turning their back on the real, the jurors for being so naïve, the courts for even trying the case, the police for arresting him, and his old girl for not being strong enough to hold shit down when she was supposed to.

He was mad at himself for loving family members who let him down and the ones who loved him. Rayven was just mad. *Why would God punish me?*

Rayven thought of the niggas who left him for dead. He had missed out on a lot of good relationships. The world was fucked up at that moment. The last thing he remembered as he fell asleep was being mad and hoping he would feel better in the morning.

Chapter 10

Buttons' Life seemed to be spiraling out of control. Christmas was just a few days away, and it had been two weeks since she had been taken in for questioning. The two detectives were still trying to get her to talk. Six Nine was being held on the women's side of the Baltimore City Jail with no bail on attempted murder and handgun charges. As it turned out, Trina's brother had slipped out of his coma and started singing like an old R&B artist looking to make a comeback and go platinum.

"This is it right here," Keisha whispered to Buttons as they came upon East Eager Street in an Uber. "I came to see my cousin over here a few times with my mother."

Looking at the smoke-gray castle-looking building, Buttons spoke. "You can let us out right here."

The waiting line to enter the jail looked crazy long. *Damn, everybody locked up. That's why I can't find a good man,* Keisha thought.

Buttons and Keisha got out of the Uber with the clothing package that they had for Six Nine. She had requested underclothes, earphones, and tennis, all of which they had. They walked up and got in line. The line was full of women and children. There were a few men but mostly women. Buttons and Keisha started talking to pass the time until they got to the registration window.

"Girl, you know my credit ain't shit," Keisha replied in response to Buttons' question about getting a cell phone.

"It can't be worse than mine," Buttons assured her.

Keisha started laughing. "Are you crazy? Girl, by the time I was ten, my mother had phones, Wifi, cable, and all kinds of other shit in my name."

"Damn, Keis. Your credit fucked up." Buttons had to give her that.

"Next!"

"Oh, that's us." Keisha and Buttons got up, crossing the line and leaving the other visitors five feet behind.

"Good afternoon, ladies. Name and number of the person you are here to see." The male officer was eyeing them.

Keisha looked in her handbag for the information.

Buttons looked at the officer who looked like he was annoyed by them. *What the fuck is his problem?*

"Oh, here it is." Keisha smiled, pulling out a piece of folded paper. "Girl, I was about to say I forgot it."

"What's his name and number?" he asked again, showing more of his antagonism toward them.

"Her name is Latisha Hartmond, Number 0-0-9-2-3-3-5-8-1-7," Keisha read from the paper, knowing the officer felt stupid.

"Oh." He smiled. "My bad. I just get so tired of seeing beautiful women wasting their time and life on these losers when a man like me is out here working hard."

Buttons wondered how many women went for that bullshit.

Keisha had to respond. She had been through this before.

"Well, I'm tired of men like you trying to prey on weak women when their man is locked up. It's like y'all can't wait until a real man is locked up, but ask yourself this. If we ain't want you while they were out here, why would we want you now?" *Keisha checked him.* "Now you have a nice day."

Buttons gave the joker their ID cards and passed through the gates after dropping the package in a drop box.

"Did you see the look on his face?" Keisha knew she had put him in his lame ass place.

“Did I?” Buttons was laughing, thinking of the clown in the registration booth.

“He must be one of those dudes that got chased home from school.”

“Or one of them chumps who lost his girl to a thug ass nigga.” Buttons laughed even harder. She felt sorry that he had to use his job as a form of revenge.

“Whatever his issue is, he needs to know that Keisha does them all. The good, the bad, even mamma’s boys, but she doesn’t do rats, police, or suckers. I hate bitch ass niggas like him.”

“Hey, girl,” they said in unison after Six Nine sat down in front of them.

“Hey.” Six Nine smiled. “So what’s good?”

“Ain’t shit. We trying to figure out what the fuck is going on,” Keisha spoke.

Buttons kept looking around. She couldn’t believe that all these women were locked up.

Babies were crying out for their mothers, and Buttons could hear bits and pieces of people’s conversations.

“So, he ain’t stopping past the house with the lawyer money?”

“Where are my children?”

“Niggas ain’t shit!”

“Fuck that bitch!”

“I can’t do no twenty years.”

“So my baby father is blaming that shit on me?”

“See if grandma will put up the house for me.”

“Trina’s bitch ass brother is snitching,” Six Nine fired, bringing Buttons’ attention back to the conversation. “Turns out that he’s a CI. He ratted on some dudes from Gilmore Street named Lil’ Melvin and J-Roc, I think. This chick on the section knows his whole family.”

“What the fuck is a CI?” Keisha questioned.

Buttons was also curious. *It’s probably some shit like ‘Cheese Industry’* Buttons joked to herself.

"A CI is the nickname for a confidential informant. Simply put, he works as an undercover for the police."

"Damn. Is that bad?" Buttons leaned forward.

"It could be."

"But he's not even dead. Plus, it was self-defense anyway," Keisha said.

"Yeah, but he's one of theirs, and this time, pain was hungrier than death, so he better count his blessings." Six Nine remembered to clear something. "Y'all know what's so funny?"

"What?"

"According to the statement of charges, there's only one statement, and it's from the victim."

"What does that mean?" Buttons asked.

"Nobody else gave a statement." Six Nine knew they got the point. All the Four Horsemen held strong. "The public defender is requesting the discovery this coming week."

Discovery and all that other legal talk were foreign to Buttons and Keisha, so they just took Six Nine's word for it. All they needed to know was that nobody was telling. They told Six Nine about the detectives and the statements they had given, or the lack thereof.

"That's cool. That's what I told you to do," Six Nine said after Buttons informed her of how she choked up under the pressure. Six Nine knew she was new to this.

They talked about everything and promised to send Six Nine some holiday photos.

Buttons was curious about everything. She told them about the dude she was trading thoughts with. Six Nine talked about how a day in jail went. They were tripping. Yusra and Nichelle's names came up for a minute, as did Keisha's brother.

"Fuck all that," Keisha cut Buttons off from talking about her friend. "Six, I know you miss that dick when you get horny and shit."

Maybe I'm giving Rayven too much. Shit! I only got one letter, but shit! He sound realer than any nigga I have ever fucked with, Buttons thought for a long second and then decided to take Keisha's advice. "Bitch! She can still play with that pussy. Ain't that right, girl?" Buttons knew she would be playing with her shit.

"Do you share a room with somebody?"

"Nah. It's an eighty man, or rather women dorm, but just so you know, I got a little bun." Six Nine blushed.

"A bun?" Keisha repeated to be sure.

Buttons looked at Keisha to make sure she heard right before looking at Six Nine. She was a sexy, caramel-complexion-skinned chick with long, jet-black, wet and wavy-looking hair. Six Nine reminded people of basketball legend Kelsey Plum. She had to be the girl.

"You're not the aggressor, are you?"

"Why wouldn't I be? I have been bisexual since high school."

"You're playing. Why you ain't never tell me?" Keisha didn't believe her.

"For what? Girl, please. Anyway, my little bun is bad. She's nineteen and got mad ass, but her head game is off the hook. I am still teaching her the way around a pussy." Six Nine smiled her signature sexy smile. "Her fake ass boyfriend left her for dead, like most of them suckers do. You wouldn't believe how many ride-or-die bitches get left behind. Only a real thorough nigga gonna hold a bitch down on her ride."

Buttons looked at Six Nine in a new light as she thought about the waiting line outside.

"How do y'all do it in a dorm?"

"I put my blanket over her head. Sometimes I let her eat my pussy in the shower." Six Nine felt her pussy heat up at that thought. "I be blazing her too."

"Oh." Buttons pictured the dorm. "Y'all crazy in there."

"Nah. We are just taking care of each other."

"Hartmond! Five minutes!" the officer called.

"Look, I love y'all." Six Nine was glad they came down.

"We will try to get down here a few times a month," Keisha said.

"Yeah," Buttons followed up.

"Okay, and bring Yusra and Nichelle through too."

"I got you," Keisha said. "Oh yeah. Before I forget, we brought the package."

"Good lookin' out."

"Time, Hartmond!"

"Love you," Buttons and Keisha said in unison as they got up to leave.

"Love y'all too. And give my love to the family," Six Nine said as they made their way out of the visiting room. *Buttons got a nice little ass. Being in jail could make you start to pay attention to shit that you never paid attention to before. She's lucky she's family.* Six Nine smiled to herself.

* * * * *

Buttons had been learning a lot of things over the last few weeks about jail and prison. Both Six Nine and Rayven had been taking her to school. She had been curious about jail since getting locked up. She told Rayven everything about her life. He was her safe haven. He wasn't judgmental but still expressed great concern. He almost seemed too good to be true. Buttons was still working at the strip club and planned on moving out of her mother's house right after graduation. Rayven was helping her so much. School was going good. She was back on track with her credits and stuff. Plus, she had talked Keisha into coming back right after New Year's. The worst was over.

"Hello, Ms. Howard."

Buttons was making her way across the school parking lot. "I don't have anything to say." Buttons looked at the two detectives sitting in the tinted window of the skin-blue Crown Victoria.

"Why you wanna play it like that, Ms. Howard?" one of them asked.

"Yeah?" the other called behind her.

Buttons paid them no mind as she kept making her way to the waiting car.

"What's up?" Yusra said when Buttons got in the car with her, Keisha, and Nichelle. "Shit! Them sucker ass pet detectives still fucking with me."

"What? They came up here today?" Keisha asked. She hadn't seen them when she exited the school building.

"They're right over there in that Crown Vic." Buttons pointed the car out to them.

"Hold up." Keisha jumped from the passenger seat.

They watched as she made her way over to the car and tapped on the tinted driver's window. Keisha started talking when the window rolled down. She was rolling her neck. While one hand never left her hip, her hand and fingers moved like crazy. They knew she was telling them off.

"What did you say?" Buttons questioned when Keisha returned to the car.

"I told them that if they don't leave us alone, I will have a lawyer file both harassment and sexual harassment charges."

"That's my girl," Nichelle said and started the car.

"You are crazy, girl." Yusra shook her head at Keisha.

"Nah. These bitches are trying to make a motherfucker talk." Keisha didn't like that they kept going at Buttons. "Even when you don't want to. Shit! I know it's their job, but damn!"

"Nichelle, drive over to Sliver Moon's." Keisha was jive hungry. Sliver Moon was a popular carry-out on Baltimore Street where everybody in the city ate. Their food was like that.

"You're always hungry," Nichelle said, but she wanted something herself.

"Yeah, do that." Yusra rubbed her stomach like she hadn't eaten less than two hours ago. "I'm on E too."

"I know a nigga who can fill up your tank." Nichelle laughed.

"Bitch! Don't play with me!" Yusra barked, more than serious. Nichelle made her sick at times. "My man does just fine, hooker."

"That man of yours is fine," Keisha added, smiling, breaking the tension.

"Oh yeah, Keisha. Dewey said to give him a call," Buttons spoke. She had seen him two days before.

"That nigga hooked on this pussy." Keisha knew she had the nigga gone.

"Bitch, please. He probably hooked on that ass or head because I don't think your pussy that good," Nichelle said.

"You wanna taste it? Because, girl, you—"

"Oh my God! Look at that fine ass nigga right there!" Buttons screamed as they were driving down Baltimore Street, and she saw a dude standing at the bus stop with some chick.

"Damn. He is fine as shit." Keisha eyed the dude.

Even Yusra gave up a sexual stare and moan. "Mmmh."

"Who is that ugly bitch he all bunned up with?" Nichelle thought of pulling over to talk to the dark-chocolate dude. "I know that ain't his girl."

"Stop hating. You're always hating." Keisha looked at the chick and had to give her dues.

She wasn't ugly at all.

"Hating? Please. Hating for what?" Nichelle knew the chick was cool.

The fine ones were always taken. "She's putting it on that that nigga. I bet that."

They looked happy to Buttons.

"She better be." Yusra took one last look. "We might gang rape his butt." They all looked at Yusra and smiled. "What?" Yusra smirked.

"Mmmhmm." They all moaned.

They pulled up right outside of Sliver Moon after Nichelle made a left off Baltimore Street onto Free Mount Street. They hopped out and made their way inside after Nichelle parked the car.

"Damn, that chicken smell good," Keisha said when they stepped inside the carry-out.

"What are you getting? I'm getting a chicken box," Nichelle said, reading Keisha's mind.

"I don't know for sure yet. A chicken box does sound good." Keisha continued to look up and read over the menu.

Yusra stepped up to the end of the line. "I know what I want. Buttons, do you want something?"

"Nah. I'm good. I ate in school."

The line wasn't as long as usual, because it was still early in the day. It was just after five o'clock, but the winter sky made it appear later.

"Can I have two double cheeseburgers with lettuce, tomatoes, mayonnaise, ketchup, salt, pepper, and extra cheese. Give me a large order of fries, and a half and half (iced tea and lemonade)," Yusra spoke to the heavy-set, older black woman, whom everyone looked at like a mother.

"Yusra, I told you I'm cool. I ate at school." Buttons wasn't full, but she was far from hungry.

"I didn't get you anything. This is all me." Yusra rolled her eyes.

"Will that be all?" the heavy-set woman asked.

"Yes, ma'am."

She called Yusra's order out to the cook through a square-shaped window and gave Yusra her order number.

"May I help you?"

"Yeah. Let me get one chicken box covered in gravy. A cheese steak sub…" Nichelle paused for a second. "Keis, you want hots on your sub?"

"No!" Keisha yelled from outside the carry-out. Nichelle turned back around and continued to order. "No hots…"

"You will be number forty-one."

Nichelle took the number from the older woman and walked out front with her girls.

"You been fucking with them prison niggas too much."

They were out front, talking about dudes being in shape, when Nichelle walked outside. People were coming and going. All kinds of cars were riding past.

"No. That's not it. I just like men who are in shape. I don't see you running around with no fat boy either," Keisha responded to Yusra.

"What are y'all beefing about now?" Nichelle wanted in on the topic.

"She's talking about I'm shallow because I want a man who has it going on."

"That's not what I said," Yusra defended.

"You did say that." Keisha looked to Buttons for support.

"What did she say?"

"I ain't getting in it." Buttons put both hands up.

"You started it!" Yusra barked.

"I ain't start shit! All I said was that my baby Rayven was cut up like a bag of dope."

"I know that's right!" Nichelle high-fived her. She couldn't wait to add her two cents. "Ain't nothing wrong with a fine, cut-up man with a big ol' piece of pipe."

"I never said it was," Yusra assured her.

"Yes, you did," Keisha corrected.

"I never said that. I said you shouldn't always base your relationship on looks and penis size."

"Dick size, Queen Elizabeth. Tell her the rest," Keisha jumped in. Buttons was laughing so hard that tears started to fall from her eyes.

"And I said that most of the time, only black men who have been to prison worry about six packs and stuff."

"What about white boys? You know, I think you might need a white boy," Nichelle added.

"You are so hard on the brothers." Nichelle had just taken it somewhere else.

"First of all, I don't want no damn white man. Unlike you, I have a fine, strong, educated black man at home. And I am hard on black men because they are so much better than what they settle for. They are worth so much more. Black men—our black men—are supposed to guide us, not use us. They are supposed to protect and educate us, not intentionally hurt us. I know they are not perfect, but some things, I don't understand. I am very proud to be a black woman who knows how to let her black man take the lead so I can follow him. What about you? Do you even know your history, Nichelle? Do you know what power you have as a black woman?" She had hit a nerve. Yusra was going off.

"I know enough to know how to make these niggas spend their money on me, while you continue to go from job to job." Nichelle was fighting back.

"Yeah, but at what cost? What does it cost you to empty a *nigga's* pockets, as you say?" Nichelle remained quiet, so Yusra continued. "Women like you are poison to our men. They are using y'all against our men, just like the devil used Eve to get Adam. Men are at our mercy, yet they are our strength. Women like me need to step up and take control."

"Don't bring the Holy Qur'an into your little game," Nichelle had to fire back.

"The Holy Qur'an? You don't have a clue." Everybody knew that Yusra was the most conscious out of the crew. "Oh, you want me to quote the Bible, the same book they used to enslave my people? I bet you still think Adam was the first man, right? Well, let me educate you, girlfriend. In the old dictionary, before it was rewritten, it tells you that the non-European was the first man to walk this earth." Yusra was ready for debate.

"Y'all, come on now," Buttons finally said. She had let it go on long enough. She didn't want to get started. She loved her history and felt like she could challenge Yusra, but she liked when she belittled Nichelle. "Give me your ticket. They called your number by now."

Yusra handed Buttons her ticket. "Nichelle, ain't your number forty-one?"

"Yeah."

"Well, you can walk with me. If they called her, I'm sure they called you too."

"Why did you get her started?" Buttons questioned as they walked up to the counter.

"Forty."

Buttons passed the heavyset lady the ticket. "You know you and Yusra ain't the best of friends."

"I ain't start with her," Nichelle defended herself.

"Yes, you did. You've been jigging at her since I got in the car."

Nichelle smiled. "You know I got love for her ass. I just like getting her hyped up. It ain't my fault that I can get under her skin."

"Girl, you're crazy. You need to stop. I will meet you out front."

"Forty-one."

"Excuse me," Buttons said to two guys blocking the doorway as they talked. *Why can't he just step outside with his friend and talk? People are so rude.*

Glocup, glocup, glocup, glocup, glocup!

Shots rang out right in front of Buttons. She and the dude in the doorway both rushed to re-enter the carry-out at the same time. Bullets were flying, hitting the door panels and everybody in their path. There were no names on them, and anybody was a target.

Buttons was looking at Nichelle with the fear of God in her eyes just before she went down. “Ahhh!”

It was like the shots would never stop. What seemed like minutes was only seconds.

Nichelle was trying to shield herself from the flying bullets in the corner when the shots stopped. Nichelle looked up and then got up and rushed over to Buttons, whom she had watched fall. “Oh my God! Buttons! Keisha, help me!” Nichelle looked around for help. Buttons was covered in blood. Blood was coming from her head. She was lying in the doorway next to the guy who tried to rush back in with her. At that moment, Nichelle realized that her girls were nowhere in sight.

“Keis! Yusra!” She jumped up and stepped over Buttons and the guy to get outside. “Keisha! Yusra! Oh my God!” What she saw made her stomach turn, and she instantly started throwing up. “Oh God! Help me! Someone help me!” Nichelle was so gone that she didn’t notice one of her girls move and whisper for help.

“Help me, please!”

* * * * *

Rayven was about to come off of lock-up soon. He was ready to get on the phone. He had plans to mail Buttons his transcripts. He was feeling her like that. They were sharing thoughts, and Rayven wanted to keep it real with her.

“Man, fuck that bitch ass nigga!” Rayven was talking to Moon about Marlboro. “Them little niggas out there don’t want no real drama like that. It’s all or nothing with me. I don’t know how to turn off halfway through.”

Word had been floating around the compound that Marlboro had put a hit on Rayven’s head for six grams of blow (dope), which was a heavy price in prison.

“You never know, Slim.” Moon knew that times were changing. The young dudes were more radical, always looking to earn a name for themselves. They didn't respect anything but knife play, and a lot of them would snitch if shit got real grimy, thus making them all the more dangerous. It was hard to beat a go-hard rat. Extermination was the only option.

"I ain't saying I can't be touched." Rayven knew only a fool thought like that. "I'm just saying that if a nigga hit me, he better lay me down. I earned all my bones the hard way. I've been on both sides of the knife. On my dead man, I will take these niggas to another level of war."

"I'm sending Marlboro a kite and letting him know that if he pushes that hit, all bets are off." Moon would go hard about the man he looked at like family.

"Nah. Fuck that nigga. Never reveal your hand. If he wants to play it like that, then it's on." Rayven's mind started working. "Come closer," he whispered. "Just chill until I come off. Let's see what happens. It might just be a rumor. If something jumps, then it's war."

"What do you want me to do?"

"Just make sure that you have me something nasty waiting when I come off lock-up."

Lock Down Publications and Ca$h Presents
Assisted Publishing Packages

Due to an increase in the price of services we have increased our prices. The prices below reflect the price increase as of 11/1/24.

BASIC PACKAGE **$699** Editing Cover Design Formatting	**UPGRADED PACKAGE** **$1000** Typing Editing Cover Design Formatting Upload eBooks to Amazon Upload Paperback to Amazon
ADVANCE PACKAGE **$1,400** Typing Editing (line editing/content) Cover Design Formatting Copyright Registration Proofreading Upload eBooks to Amazon Upload Paperback to Amazon	**LDP SUPREME PACKAGE** **$1,700** Typing Editing (line editing/content) Cover Design Formatting Copyright Registration Proofreading Set up Amazon Account Upload eBooks to Amazon Upload Paperback to Amazon Advertise on LDP's Amazon and Facebook Page

***

Other services available upon request.
Additional charges may apply

Lock Down Publications
P.O. Box 944
Stockbridge, GA 30281-9998
Phone: 470 303-9761
Email: lockdownpublications@gmail.com

Submission Guideline

Submit the first three chapters of your completed manuscript to ldpsubmissions@gmail.com. In the subject line add **Your Book's Title**. The manuscript must be in a Word Doc file and sent as an attachment. Document should be in Times New Roman, double spaced, and in size 12 font. Also, provide your synopsis and full contact information. If sending multiple submissions, they must each be in a separate email.

Have a story but no way to send it electronically? You can still submit to LDP/Ca$h Presents. Send in the first three chapters, written or typed, of your completed manuscript to:

LDP: Submissions Dept
P.O. Box 944
Stockbridge, GA 30281-9998

DO NOT send original manuscript. Must be a duplicate. Provide your synopsis and a cover letter containing your full contact information.

Thanks for considering LDP and Ca$h Presents.

NEW RELEASES

BLOODLINE OF A SAVAGE 1-3
THESE VICIOUS STREETS 1-3
RELENTLESS GOON 1-3
BY PRINCE A. TAUHID

THE BUTTERFLY MAFIA 1-3
BY FUMIYA PAYNE

A THUG'S STREET PRINCESS 1&2
BY MEESHA

CITY OF SMOKE 3
BY MOLOTTI

GET IT IN SLUGS 1 &2
BY B. STALL

STANDING ON HER BUSINESS 1&2
BY DG SANTANA

STEPPERS 1,2&3
THE REAL BADDIES OF CHI-RAQ
BY KING RIO

THE LANE 1&2
BY KEN-KEN SPENCE

THUG OF SPADES 1&2
LOVE IN THE TRENCHES 2
CORNER BOYS
BY COREY ROBINSON

TIL DEATH 3
BY ARYANNA

THE BIRTH OF A GANGSTER 4
BY DELMONT PLAYER

PRODUCT OF THE STREETS 1-3
BY DEMOND "MONEY" ANDERSON

NO TIME FOR ERROR
BY KEESE

MONEY HUNGRY DEMONS 1-2
BY TRANAY ADAMS

HUB CITY MENACE 1-3
BY J. WHITE

A THUGGISH PASSION 1&2
LAND OF DA HOOLIGANZ 1-4
KILLAZ ON STANDBY 1&2
BY IRA B.

FO'EVA ROLLIN 1&2
BY ASSA RAYMOND BAKER

THE LEVEL UP 1&3
BY LUXURY KING

Coming Soon from Lock Down Publications/Ca$h Presents

IF YOU CROSS ME ONCE 6
ANGEL V
By Anthony Fields

A THUGS STREET PRINCESS 3
By Meesha

CORNER BOYS 2
By Corey Robinson

THA TAKEOVER
By Keith Chandler

BETRAYAL OF A G 2
By Ray Vinci

SAVAGE FAMILY EMPIRE 1&2
SOULLESS GOON 1,2&3
THE DIRTY SIDE OF MONEY 1,2&3
By Prince

FOR MY ENEMY'S SAKE
AMBITIONS OF A SLIDER
FRESH OFF DA PORCH
By IRA B.

BY THE TRUCKLOAD 1-4
TIPPIN' THE SCALES 1-3
BAD BITCHES WIT GUNZ 3
PROBLEM SOLVED 2
By Christopher "Diesel" Hornezes

Available Now

RESTRAINING ORDER 1 & 2
By **CA$H & Coffee**

LOVE KNOWS NO BOUNDARIES 1-3
By **Coffee**

RAISED AS A GOON I, II, III & IV
BRED BY THE SLUMS I, II, III
BLAST FOR ME I & II
ROTTEN TO THE CORE I II III
A BRONX TALE I, II, III
DUFFLE BAG CARTEL I II III IV V VI
HEARTLESS GOON I II III IV V
A SAVAGE DOPEBOY I II
DRUG LORDS I II III
CUTTHROAT MAFIA I II
KING OF THE TRENCHES
By **Ghost**

LAY IT DOWN I & II
LAST OF A DYING BREED I II
BLOOD STAINS OF A SHOTTA I & II III
By **Jamaica**

LOYAL TO THE GAME I II III
LIFE OF SIN I, II III
By **TJ & Jelissa**

IF LOVING HIM IS WRONG…I & II
LOVE ME EVEN WHEN IT HURTS I II III
By **Jelissa**

PUSH IT TO THE LIMIT
By **Bre' Hayes**

BLOODY COMMAS I & II
SKI MASK CARTEL I, II & III
KING OF NEW YORK I II, III IV V
RISE TO POWER I II III
COKE KINGS I II III IV V
BORN HEARTLESS I II III IV
KING OF THE TRAP I II
By **T.J. Edwards**

WHEN THE STREETS CLAP BACK I & II III
THE HEART OF A SAVAGE I II III IV
MONEY MAFIA I II
LOYAL TO THE SOIL I II III
By **Jibril Williams**

A DISTINGUISHED THUG STOLE MY HEART I II & III
LOVE SHOULDN'T HURT I II III IV
RENEGADE BOYS 1-4
PAID IN KARMA 1-3
SAVAGE STORMS 1-3
AN UNFORESEEN LOVE 1-3
BABY, I'M WINTERTIME COLD 1-3
A THUG'S STREET PRINCESS 1&2
By **Meesha**

A GANGSTER'S CODE 1-3
A GANGSTER'S SYN 1-3
THE SAVAGE LIFE 1-3
CHAINED TO THE STREETS 1-3
BLOOD ON THE MONEY 1-3
A GANGSTA'S PAIN 1-3
BEAUTIFUL LIES AND UGLY TRUTHS
CHURCH IN THESE STREETS
By **J-Blunt**

CUM FOR ME 1-8
An LDP Erotica Collaboration

BLOOD OF A BOSS 1-5
SHADOWS OF THE GAME
TRAP BASTARD
By **Askari**

THE STREETS BLEED MURDER 1-3
THE HEART OF A GANGSTA 1-3
By **Jerry Jackson**

WHEN A GOOD GIRL GOES BAD
By **Adrienne**

THE COST OF LOYALTY 1-3
By **Kweli**

BRIDE OF A HUSTLA 1-3
THE FETTI GIRLS 1-3
CORRUPTED BY A GANGSTA 1-4
BLINDED BY HIS LOVE
THE PRICE YOU PAY FOR LOVE 1-3
DOPE GIRL MAGIC 1-3
By **Destiny Skai**

A KINGPIN'S AMBITION
A KINGPIN'S AMBITION II
I MURDER FOR THE DOUGH
By **Ambitious**

TRUE SAVAGE 1-7
DOPE BOY MAGIC 1-3
MIDNIGHT CARTEL 1-3
CITY OF KINGZ 1&2
NIGHTMARE ON SILENT AVE
THE PLUG OF LIL MEXICO 1&2
CLASSIC CITY
By **Chris Green**

A GANGSTER'S REVENGE 1-4
THE BOSS MAN'S DAUGHTERS 1-5
A SAVAGE LOVE 1&2
BAE BELONGS TO ME 1&2
A HUSTLER'S DECEIT 1-3
WHAT BAD BITCHES DO 1-3
SOUL OF A MONSTER 1-3
KILL ZONE
A DOPE BOY'S QUEEN 1-3
TIL DEATH 1-3
IMMA DIE BOUT MINE 1-6
DYING FOR LIKES
By **Aryanna**

A DOPEBOY'S PRAYER
By **Eddie "Wolf" Lee**

THE KING CARTEL 1-3
By **Frank Gresham**

THESE NIGGAS AIN'T LOYAL 1-3
By **Nikki Tee**

GANGSTA SHYT 1-3
By **CATO**

THE ULTIMATE BETRAYAL
By **Phoenix**

BOSS'N UP 1-3
By **Royal Nicole**

I LOVE YOU TO DEATH
By **Destiny J**

I RIDE FOR MY HITTA
I STILL RIDE FOR MY HITTA
By **Misty Holt**

LOVE & CHASIN' PAPER
By **Qay Crockett**

TO DIE IN VAIN
SINS OF A HUSTLA
By **ASAD**

BROOKLYN HUSTLAZ
By **Boogsy Morina**

BROOKLYN ON LOCK 1 & 2
By **Sonovia**

GANGSTA CITY
By T**eddy Duke**

A DRUG KING AND HIS DIAMOND 1-3
A DOPEMAN'S RICHES
HER MAN, MINE'S TOO 1&2
CASH MONEY HO'S
THE WIFEY I USED TO BE 1&2
PRETTY GIRLS DO NASTY THINGS
By **Nicole Goosby**

LIPSTICK KILLAH 1-3
CRIME OF PASSION 1-3
FRIEND OR FOE 1-3
By **Mimi**

TRAPHOUSE KING 1-3
KINGPIN KILLAZ 1-3
STREET KINGS 1&2
PAID IN BLOOD 1&2
CARTEL KILLAZ 1-3
DOPE GODS 1&2
By **Hood Rich**

THE STREETS ARE CALLING
By **Duquie Wilson**

STEADY MOBBN' 1-3
THE STREETS STAINED MY SOUL 1-3
By **Marcellus Allen**

WHO SHOT YA 1-3
SON OF A DOPE FIEND 1-4
HEAVEN GOT A GHETTO 1&2
SKI MASK MONEY 1&2
By **Renta**

GORILLAZ IN THE BAY 1-4
TEARS OF A GANGSTA 1/&2
3X KRAZY 1&2
STRAIGHT BEAST MODE 1&2
By **DE'KARI**

TRIGGADALE 1-3
MURDA WAS THE CASE 1-3
By **Elijah R. Freeman**

SLAUGHTER GANG 1-3
RUTHLESS HEART 1-3
By **Willie Slaughter**

GOD BLESS THE TRAPPERS 1-3
THESE SCANDALOUS STREETS 1-3
FEAR MY GANGSTA 1-5
THESE STREETS DON'T LOVE NOBODY 1-2
BURY ME A G 1-5
A GANGSTA'S EMPIRE 1-4
THE DOPEMAN'S BODYGAURD 1&2
THE REALEST KILLAZ 1-3
THE LAST OF THE OGS 1-3
By **Tranay Adams**

MARRIED TO A BOSS 1-3
By **Destiny Skai & Chris Green**

KINGZ OF THE GAME 1-7
CRIME BOSS 1-4
By **Playa Ray**

FUK SHYT
By **Blakk Diamond**

DON'T F#CK WITH MY HEART 1&2
By **Linnea**

ADDICTED TO THE DRAMA 1-3
IN THE ARM OF HIS BOSS
By **Jamila**

LOYALTY AIN'T PROMISED 1&2
By **Keith Williams**

YAYO 1-4
A SHOOTER'S AMBITION 1&2
BRED IN THE GAME
By **S. Allen**

TRAP GOD 1-3
RICH $AVAGE 1-3
MONEY IN THE GRAVE 1-3
CARTEL MONEY 1&2
By **Martell Troublesome Bolden**

FOREVER GANGSTA 1&2
GLOCKS ON SATIN SHEETS 1&2
By **Adrian Dulan**

TOE TAGZ 1-4
LEVELS TO THIS SHYT 1&2
IT'S JUST ME AND YOU
By **Ah'Million**

KINGPIN DREAMS 1-3
RAN OFF ON DA PLUG
By **Paper Boi Rari**

THE STREETS MADE ME 1-3
By **Larry D. Wright**

CONFESSIONS OF A GANGSTA 1-4
CONFESSIONS OF A JACKBOY 1-3
CONFESSIONS OF A HITMAN
CONFESSIONS OF A DOPE BOY
By **Nicholas Lock**

I'M NOTHING WITHOUT HIS LOVE
SINS OF A THUG
TO THE THUG I LOVED BEFORE
A GANGSTA SAVED XMAS
IN A HUSTLER I TRUST
By **Monet Dragun**

QUIET MONEY 1-3
THUG LIFE 1-3
EXTENDED CLIP 1&2
A GANGSTA'S PARADISE
By **Trai'Quan**

CAUGHT UP IN THE LIFE 1-3
THE STREETS NEVER LET GO 1-3
By **Robert Baptiste**

NEW TO THE GAME 1-3
MONEY, MURDER & MEMORIES 1-3
By **Malik D. Rice**

CREAM 2-3
THE STREETS WILL TALK
By **Yolanda Moore**

THE STREETS WILL NEVER CLOSE 1-3
By **K'ajji**

LIFE OF A SAVAGE 1-4
A GANGSTA'S QUR'AN 1-4
MURDA SEASON 1-3
GANGLAND CARTEL 1-3
CHI'RAQ GANGSTAS 1-4
KILLERS ON ELM STREET 1-3
JACK BOYZ N DA BRONX 1-3
A DOPEBOY'S DREAM 1-3
JACK BOYS VS DOPE BOYS 1-3
COKE GIRLZ
COKE BOYS
SOSA GANG 1&2
BRONX SAVAGES
BODYMORE KINGPINS
BLOOD OF A GOON
By **Romell Tukes**

CONCRETE KILLA 1-3
VICIOUS LOYALTY 1-3
BLOODY MONEY BAGS
By **Kingpen**

THE ULTIMATE SACRIFICE 1-6
KHADIFI
IF YOU CROSS ME ONCE 1-3
ANGEL 1-4
IN THE BLINK OF AN EYE
By **Anthony Fields**

THE LIFE OF A HOOD STAR
By **Ca$h & Rashia Wilson**

NIGHTMARES OF A HUSTLA 1-3
BLOOD AND GAMES 1&2
By **King Dream**

GHOST MOB
By **Stilloan Robinson**

HARD AND RUTHLESS 1&2
MOB TOWN 251
THE BILLIONAIRE BENTLEYS 1-3
REAL G'S MOVE IN SILENCE
By **Von Diesel**

MOB TIES 1-7
SOUL OF A HUSTLER, HEART OF A KILLER 1-3
GORILLAZ IN THE TRENCHES
OOPS CRY TOO 1&2
THE DAUGHTER OF A CARTEL BOSS
By **SayNoMore**

BODYMORE MURDERLAND 1-3
THE BIRTH OF A GANGSTER 1-4
By **Delmont Player**

FOR THE LOVE OF A BOSS 1&2
By **C. D. Blue**

KILLA KOUNTY 1-5
TENDER
By **Khufu**

MOBBED UP 1-4
THE BRICK MAN 1-5
THE COCAINE PRINCESS 1-10
STEPPERS 1-3
SUPER GREMLIN 1-4
A GANGSTA'S SON
By **King Rio**

MONEY GAME 1&2
By **Smoove Dolla**

A GANGSTA'S KARMA 1-5
By **FLAME**

KING OF THE TRENCHES 1-3
By **GHOST & TRANAY ADAMS**

BAD BITCHES WIT GUNZ 1&2
PROBLEM SOLVED
By "Christopher Diesel" Hornezes

QUEEN OF THE ZOO 1&2
By **Black Migo**

GRIMEY WAYS 1-3
BETRAYAL OF A G
By **Ray Vinci**

XMAS WITH AN ATL SHOOTER
By **Ca$h & Destiny Skai**

KING KILLA 1&2
By **Vincent "Vitto" Holloway**

BETRAYAL OF A THUG 1&2
By **Fre$h**

COUNTDOWN OF A KILLA 1&2
SEX, MURDER AND GOD 1&2
GUNS DOWN, BOTTOMS UP 1&2
By Lo-Life

THE MURDER QUEENS 1-7
By **Michael Gallon**

FOR THE LOVE OF BLOOD 1-4
By **Jamel Mitchell**

HOOD CONSIGLIERE 1&2
NO TIME FOR ERROR
By **Keese**

PROTÉGÉ OF A LEGEND 1,2&3
LOVE IN THE TRENCHES 1&2
By **Corey Robinson**

THE PLUG'S RUTHLESS DAUGHTER 1&2
By **Tony Daniels**

BORN IN THE GRAVE 1-3
CRIME PAYS
By **Self Made Tay**

MOAN IN MY MOUTH
By **XTASY**

TORN BETWEEN A GANGSTER AND A GENTLEMAN
By **J-BLUNT & Miss Kim**

LOYALTY IS EVERYTHING 1-3
CITY OF SMOKE 1-3
By **Molotti**

HERE TODAY GONE TOMORROW 1&2
By **Fly Rock**

WOMEN LIE MEN LIE 1-4
FIFTY SHADES OF SNOW 1-3
STACK BEFORE YOU SPLURGE
GIRLS FALL LIKE DOMINOES
NAÏVE TO THE STREETS
By **ROY MILLIGAN**

PILLOW PRINCESS
By **S. Hawkins**

THE BUTTERFLY MAFIA 1-3
SALUTE MY SAVAGERY 1&2
By **Fumiya Payne**

THE LANE 1&2
By Ken-Ken Spence

THE PUSSY TRAP 1-5
By **Nene Capri**

DIRTY DNA
By **Blaque**

SANCTIFIED AND HORNY
by **XTASY**

BOOKS BY LDP'S CEO, CA$H

TRUST IN NO MAN
TRUST IN NO MAN 2
TRUST IN NO MAN 3
BONDED BY BLOOD
SHORTY GOT A THUG
THUGS CRY
THUGS CRY 2
THUGS CRY 3
TRUST NO BITCH
TRUST NO BITCH 2
TRUST NO BITCH 3
TIL MY CASKET DROPS
RESTRAINING ORDER
RESTRAINING ORDER 2
IN LOVE WITH A CONVICT
LIFE OF A HOOD STAR
XMAS WITH AN ATL SHOOTER

www.ingramcontent.com/pod-product-compliance
Lightning Source LLC
LaVergne TN
LVHW020715110826
845149LV00012B/2280
9781971770116